The Nightlife Chronicles

II

I0653382

Taya's Plight

Shawn Flossy

A PURP Publications Original

ISBN: 978-0-9975851
ISBN-13: 978-0-9975851-5-5

First printing
Printed in the United States

DEDICATION

This one is for all the ones that prayed on someone else's downfall.

CONTENTS

Acknowledgement

I wasn't going to revisit this storyline.

Mostly because I grew tremendously from the time I wrote my freshman piece, *The Nightlife Chronicles* and the characters and premise didn't give me the same rush it once gave me. Now, I know for sure that my characters, especially Taya, aren't done telling their stories.

We explored failure, disappointment, and untrustworthiness in the original Chronicles; I'm acknowledging that my characters, just like anyone, experience growth and clarity on the other side of failure.

This time, this story is for all of us that try; anyone that has ever had to start over and rebuild. Weathering the storm is the process and, to be fair, Taya deserves to see the other side of her downfall.

I'm taking this moment to acknowledge, respect, and trust the process.

Introduction: Flash from the Past

I initially didn't even entertain the idea of meeting Mike. But after the thought roamed in my mind all day, I decided I owed it to myself to get closure. I wasn't expecting much from our conversation other than him apologizing for his actions and promising he'll never do it again. I'm uninterested in that spiel. I'd rather hear why he thought that shady bitch, Danielle, deserved the honor of sitting on my throne. Even if it was for a midday quickie.

Tonight, I dressed modestly. Slim cream slacks, sheer coral blouse, and nude suede pumps. My hair pulled tight into a slick ponytail and my face was bare. I wasn't looking to impress him anymore. I didn't need him to be infatuated with me. I wanted my explanation and my chance to tell him how I truly felt about him.

I made myself present at The Rim Bar and Grill downtown promptly at eleven. He was already there. Fully suited in a tailored name brand sport coat and slacks, as if he was about to present in a business meeting. Our greeting was cold. A cordial side hug with minimal emotion or feelings. His face was drab. Still his normal attractive self but it was bland. He had a small cut on his forehead, from our altercation at his home, that seemed to be healing.

"Before we start, I just want you to know the moment you decide to yell, scream, or put your hands on me I'm leaving." He had the audacity to tell me.

Who the hell did he think he was talking to? My face mimicked my thoughts. "I can respect that," I replied, crossing my hands over my lap.

We were seated at an open area with couches and a small coffee table as the decor. I sat directly across from him. His posture was purely professional.

"In order to give both of us the chance to feel closure, there's a few things we need to lay down on the table." I nodded in agreement.

"We can start with the lighter of the conversation topics, Danielle," he commanded.

"That's the lighter of the topics? Your pure cold-hearted adultery is the lighter topic?" I was appalled.

"I mean, that's honestly old news to me. That shit happened last month. An unfortunate experience but it's over."

"Oh, it's just over because you say it is," I snapped.

"No, it's over because it happened in the past. I got caught fucking my ex. You beat her ass. Nothing else to really discuss."

"How about we discuss why you chose to fuck that slut?"

He laughed. I scowled. "You really need me to explain why I fucked her? Where do you want me to start? With her titties or her ass?" he cynically replied.

"I want you to start with why you preached all that bullshit about us being together then your actions showed otherwise."

"I was gladly ready to call you my girl exclusively, but, as I recall, you couldn't seem to get on board with that."

"And that night I was coming over to tell you I was ready," I explained.

"Oh, so let me get this straight. Despite my many attempts to get you to be with me I still had to wait until precious Taya Roberts was ready to be cuffed? Fuck my feelings and what I wanted?"

"If I wasn't ready then I wasn't ready."

"But you seemed to be ready for Sean, Ken, and my personal favorite, Lamar. You do know that every time you got slutted out by one of those famous NBA players I received a call the next day with the play by play. I must admit, I'm impressed with how you curved KC in that hotel out in OKC. Everybody loves a ménage. But hearing how Lamar fucked you from the back busting his nut on your ass then dipped on your ass was kind of sad," he rambled.

My mouth hung low. "When I told yo ass that I knew everybody in this city I meant it. Any nigga you

11

could think of to fuck already got my number saved in their favorites."

"So you spied on me?" I was pissed.

"Hell naw. I got a whole business to run. I have no time to spy on yo ass. I just simply put it out there that I was thinking about cuffing you. And the way the guy code works is that I get reports on your behavior whenever you encounter somebody in my circle. Clearly, your little friend circle doesn't work like that." He smiled then sipped his drink.

"You're a fucking snake."

"I gave you the opportunity to be a part of my team. To be exclusively Money Mike's woman. But you'd rather be a hoe."

I sat silent for a few moments. I had to collect my thoughts and push back my emotions. "So what now?"

"Honestly, I don't know what you're going to do. But, me? I'm going back to doing all the same shit I was already doing."

"So you didn't come here today to try to get me back?" I was curious.

He laughed. And not one of those fake happy laughs, he genuinely laughed.

"You thought because you were angry at my crib the other day that I was the one in the wrong? I felt bad that you had to find out the way you did, but regardless, I was gonna have sex with her and frankly any other woman I wanted to."

"See now I'm confused. You can slut around town fucking any bitch with a fat ass but the moment I do it, it's a problem."

"The ball was in your court. I was ready to stop when you were ready to stop. But since it was clear you weren't I was prepared to continue my life. You kept going, I kept going."

I scowled then downed my entire shot. "I don't know if you noticed or not but you're not going to find a better woman in this city." I found my swag. "I was doing just fine before I met you and I'll be just fine after you." I laughed.

"I think you'll be fine. But from now on when you go anywhere you'll think about me, wish you were with me, and wonder why you didn't take your chance."

"You just some everyday dick. There will be others," I snapped back.

"Alright cool." He threw his hands up. "So you are okay with me and Camille right?"

My soul dropped. "What do you mean?" I pressed.

"Oh, she didn't tell you?"

"Tell me what, Michael?" My insides were heating up.

"She's been kicking it at the crib lately. She's been texting and calling telling me about how wrong she thinks you are. Actually, she was the key moving piece in all the information I got on you. I think I like that kind of loyalty in a female. I might have to keep her." He smiled.

My entire mood changed. I went from feeling

somewhat in control to completely losing it. "You bitch!"

"Yep and that's my cue to exit." He grabbed his phone off the table, pulled out some twenties and threw them on the table for the bill, then placed a small box on the table.

"I'm sure I'll see you around." Then he turned and walked out of the restaurant and my life.

I couldn't believe that backstabbing little bitch Camille. Smiling in my face like she was my friend but the whole time she was plotting on my man. I was boiling on the inside but had to keep some composure because people were looking over at me after my last outburst. After the waitress came by and collected the bill, I picked up the small box Mike left. Inside was a perfect hand-cut white diamond settled inside a white gold band. The engraving on the inside read: What could have been.

1

SWITCHED THE SWAG

After several years of performing and stunting on my haters in the marketing industry, I took the first exit out and ran to startup land. I had been exploring the idea for a while and plotting on some possible moves with my business partner and fellow FAMU alum, Asya Young, for way too long.

Asya spent the last eight years of her life developing software for Alcore (the same company I held my Executive Marketing position). Not only is Asya crazy talented, she's also almost a genius. She pitched the idea of developing computer software that integrates with a user's technology of choice to help improve entrepreneur customer management workflows. She was full of energy when she introduced the idea to me about a year or so ago. At the time I wasn't ready to explore new work opportunities, but with my recent misfortune, this appeared to be perfect timing. Asya knew she needed somebody with professional business acumen to take her product to the next level. Within those guidelines we agreed to fund our project 50/50.

Who would have thought I'd ever leave the sexy streets of Miami to move to Austin, TX, the new hub for startups? I know I didn't. Matter of fact, if you would have thrown the idea at me a year ago I would have likely laughed. But, boom, here I am.

With all the bullshit I went through with Michael Antonio Keith, Jr. I was through with that overly hyped ass city. And I'm especially done with, completely over, sick as hell of people asking me about Money Mike. Matter of fact, who is that? I'm not even familiar. Hell.

Just to catch you up, I spent a few weeks with Rashad in New York at the beginning of last winter. I fucked him good in those expensive hotel sheets, so good to the point where he was trying to cuff me before I hopped on a plane back home. With my record of anti-commitment, y'all know I was hesitant as hell but I went for it. I had to hand in my player card in exchange for a real nigga. Rashad actually played a huge role in my decision to move. He accepted a job offer that was literally impossible for him to refuse and he for damn sure wasn't leaving me in Florida.

So there you have it. A boss bitch switched her entire swag on y'all.

2
Power Drilled

"Taya I don't understand why you just didn't move in with Rashad." Asya opened up the convo as we unpacked our living room.

We purchased a moderate sized house out by the lake on the outskirts of Austin. Two stories, four bedrooms, three baths, crazy large lakeside backyard. More than enough space for both of us.

"Because we've only been dating for like four months. Moving in with somebody is like advancing a relationship by two years minimum," I responded.

"Wrong. This is the 21st century. We move in with our significant other for convenience."

"Convenience of what?" She had me confused.

"Dick, bitch." She laughed. I shook my head. "Plus if you live with him that makes it harder for him

17

to cheat."

"See, Asya, it was up until this very moment I wondered why you are single. Now, I get it. You've got to give niggas space. If he gone cheat he'd do it regardless if I'm around or not." I tried to school her.

"Please, Taya. Spare me that deep philosophical shit. You just got into a relationship after living yo best hoe life for a decade." She expressed herself as she stacked our bookshelf.

I rolled my eyes. "My hoe years are exactly why I can speak on this topic. You know how many niggas I fucked in their home that they shared with their girlfriends and even wives?"

"I know a few..." She corroborated my story.

"Exactly. Like I said, if he wanna cheat he will. Plus Rashad is living in the middle of the city and I wanted to live this lakeside life so... boom here we are." I finished.

There was a firm knock at the door right in the midst of our conversation. Asya looked at me but I shot her a reassuring look that I was not moving to answer.

"Oh, don't move. I'll get it." She expressed sarcasm. My face remained unmoved as I watched to see who was behind the door.

Asya peeped through the window to see who it was before opening. Our front door was off-centered to our living room with two large bay windows paired with the modern wood stained frame.

"It's some guy," she announced.

"That doesn't help, Asya." I responded. Then she opened the door.

"Hi?"

"Hey, didn't mean to disturb you. I live next door and just wanted to welcome you to the neighborhood." I heard him but I couldn't exactly see him from where I was sitting. So, I got up and joined them in the foyer.

"Oh, hi! Well, I'm Asya and this is Taya. We literally just moved in a few days ago from Florida."

Our neighbor was an approximately 6'2" tall, light skinned, bald man with a beard.

"Cool. Well welcome. I'm Callum."

Callum? He must be mixed. That's the most Caucasian name I've seen on a Black man. I extended my hand. "Taya."

"Nice to meet you. Nice to meet both of you really. Well, hey, let me know if you guys need any help. I know at some point you'll need a power drill to get those drapes and other little things done. I'm right next door."

"Wow thanks a lot. We will likely take you up on that offer." Asya finished the conversation and I made my way back to the couch. He smiled and then left.

"Well, he was nice," Asya said while closing the door.

"He just probably trying to fuck." I rolled my eyes.

"What? How did you get that from that? He was just being cordial."

"Yea cordially scoping us out. No man is that nice without an angle."

"How you don't know he's not married or something?"

"Asya. Try to keep up, please. Again. Marriage has never stopped a nigga from scoping, finding, and bagging some new pussy."

She nodded. Agreeing that I had a point. "Well regardless I'ma need him to bring that power drill over here."

"Yea just make sure he don't power drill that ass to the bed," I joked. She laughed.

I had been living in Texas for approximately three days and was officially bored out of my mind. In Miami, I would have an invite to somebody's event, party, or shindig by now. It was obvious my very first mission was to get my clout up in my new city.

Luckily, I had already unpacked my closet and room so I could get dressed to fuck shit up. Honestly, this new life and transition was all so surreal for me. I had inherited the title "That Bitch" from college and I just built upon that status as time progressed. Then, my reign came crashing down and I let the best of my ego takeover. My name still ring bells in Miami but not with the same respect. I suppose one would think I was running away from facing the truth but in reality, I was present for every last ounce of my truth. From Mike's heartbreaking confession to Camille's backstabbing ass. If anything, the truth slapped me dead in the face before I could even get my bag packed.

Now here I am, rebuilding. The last fucking

thing I thought I'd be doing at 29. Nonetheless, a rebuild offers a fresh start and the opportunity to improve my product. I had two very specific goals: the first one, get our software startup off the ground and turning around cash within the year, the second: stunt on my haters tough. Simple.

3

APPLYING FAMILIAR CONCEPTS

Breckenridge. A four-star restaurant on the outskirts of the city. Night ambiance; candlelit tables, white table clothes, polite staff, and overall well received service. A style that I am all too familiar with. My comfort zone.

"So how were your first couple days? Adjusting?" Rashad asked from across the table, looking up from his cocktail.

"I'm adjusting. A bit slower than I'm used to. I'm not exactly sure what to do with all of this new found free time." I forced a smile.

"You focus. That's what you do with it. Focus on your new goals and then actualize. Make shit happen."

"I've always been able to balance both. My goals and my nightlife."

"And, now you don't have to. Make your nightlife your new goals."

Rashad was more helpful to me than he could ever know. He never actually has intentions but is so intentional. Take for example, this particular exchange. We're here having a romantic candlelit dinner for two and he opens up small talk just to get me started, because he knows I will eventually catch a subject that sparks my interest and run with it. He has no real intentions of getting me to think, behave, or respond a certain way yet he is feeding me thoughts. He's not exactly tactical but he is extremely specific about his message. Never saying too much but always saying just enough.

"I never had Nightlife goals,." I continued.

"That's the point. You can. Figure out what exactly you want from the Nightlife."

Here he goes. Doing that thing he does when he makes me think about basic concepts. Before, I didn't have goals for my Nightlife activities; I was simply upholding my brand. A sexy sleek smart brand; a woman that got whatever it was that she wanted. But, what was it that I wanted? I suppose the shallower side of me would say I wanted sex. And, while parts of that is true, there had to be something else.

I remained quiet. Rashad gazed at me as he watched me think.

"You don't have to figure it out now but you should—"

"I have life goals. The startup and the success of it," I cut him off.

24

"And obviously you'll be busy with that which may be enough but I know you, Taya. You get bored fast."

Who told this man to read me like a book?

"Maybe it will be enough. A tech startup is no easy task," I followed.

"Pssst… please. You're a corporate tycoon. You wouldn't have even put your finger prints on it if you didn't think you could make it go." He continued to read me. I smiled.

"You're right. Asya and I are about to fuck shit up."

He laughed. "Glad we got that cleared up," he stated sarcastically.

The waiter brought out our entrees. Rashad ordered a sirloin cooked medium and loaded mashed potatoes. I was watching a well-put together masterpiece, so I ordered medium grilled salmon over an apple vinaigrette salad.

"Run the week one game plan past me one more time." Rashad was referring to my business plan. Specifically, my week one objectives.

"Boom. I meet with Catherine Winsdale next Tuesday. She's supposedly the gatekeeper on public relations as it comes to technology in this market. My only goal with her is to make her completely aware of my presence. I'm talking first name basis aware."

"You get Winsdale talking about you and you're automatically a part of every tech conversation…"

"That's exactly my M.O. Recognizing that I'm a small fish in this game at the moment and that humble actions should be my only moves in these early stages. I need all these mothafuckas to pick up what I'm throwing out."

Rashad nodded in affirmation. "And what's Asya doing?"

"Building the team. We have the prototype, the business plan, and the capital to get everything up and running. What most new startup owners struggle with the most, outside of funding, is the ability to move from idea to ideation. We won't have those problems. Asya is working on phase two now while I lock down phase one. This is our operating model. We behave like we got it, even when we don't."

"And your real estate?"

"I got it down to two locations. But, I need to find the core network and get the inside scope on prime location strategies. This is one decision I don't want to make too soon. It's hard to roll back from a real estate decision."

Rashad smiled. "No easy task you say?"

"I know it sounds like I got my shit together but this shit might get tough."

"How'd you do it back in Florida?"

"Playing suckas…" I shrugged.

"Apply that concept." Rashad laughed at first but his point was valid.

I knew Rashad could see my facial expression change as I contemplated how to execute that idea. Playing suckas for clout, money, club appearances, bottles, etc. was all I did back in Florida. I had the money to do whatever I wanted but I rarely paid for anything. Most of the time, I wasn't even fucking; just simply casually flirting, playing the game, and securing the bag. He was right. I could apply that same concept.

People, regardless of their profession, are still just people. They need love, affection, fun, and all that extra shit. With proper execution, I could make my old habits

new and improved habits and cash out in the meantime.

4

MISSION WINSDALE

"Remind me again why we're on the internet stalking this middle-aged white woman?" Asya was confused.

"Asya, for the third time, I need to do more research on this lady. Where she be outside of work and what type of stuff she's into."

"And, Taya, for the third time, this bitch is mad boring! She doesn't do shit except marketing consultations every Thursday. She's a square."

"Even squares have fun," I replied.

"No the fuck they don't. That's why we call them squares," she followed. I rolled my eyes.

"Boom. Look." I flagged Asya over to look at my laptop screen.

"A wine club?"

"Not just any wine club. This wine club has a

Facebook group."

"Ok, and? I suppose being a square gets stressful and she uses the wine to forget about her lameness."

"That Facebook group shows me that she gets wavy with these wine people every Wednesday on Wine-Wednesday."

Asya rolled her eyes. "Ok, whatever. Now what?"

"We go."

"Fuck. No! How many more times do I have to explain how lame this is?"

"I wasn't asking you if you wanted to go. I'm telling you. Go get dressed." I grabbed my laptop and headed for my room.

"What am I supposed to wear to a Square Convention? I don't own suspenders." I heard Asya complain faintly in the distance. I laughed.

I own an extensive wardrobe. Anything from Sophisticated Chic to Sassy Hoochie was present in my closet. My signature has always been my ability to pull off sexy even when sexy wasn't invited. I honestly can't help it. I wanted to come off warm and inviting at this event. I pulled out a sheer white blouse, white fitted slacks, and tan five and half inch pumps. I slicked my hair back into a ponytail, laid my edges, beat my face, and dabbed some body oil for an inviting scent.

Asya was being lackadaisical but she pulled off a professional lavender pantsuit and black suede pumps. That was her thing; be difficult but reliable all at the same time. My type of bitch.

When I left Florida, I sold my BMW and copped a Tesla. Something that said I was about this tech life but I'm still drippin' sauce. We drove from the Lakeside, through the city out to the suburbs. You know how the suburbs are; lots of majorities and a sprinkle of minorities. You have your avid joggers and the occasional over-achieving jogging mom pushing a stroller working that baby fat off. We were definitely in the right place.

"Taya this plan of yours better work or I'ma–"

"Or you gone wait for me to come up with the next plan." I cut off Asya. "Look. I get it. This is not your lane. You're use to a different space. But trust me when I tell you building this network might be the single most important critical task we have to do if we want this startup to take off. The key differentiator between Black-owned businesses and businesses lead by non-people of color is the ability to navigate and leverage a large network. We gotta do this shit. I would never steer you wrong."

Asya looked over at me with a stern face. "This is why you my bitch! Smart ass MBA having ass fine ass Black woman. You better shut me up." We laughed.

We arrived at a country club settled at the end of the suburban community we had to navigate through. I drove around the seven-foot-tall elegant water fountain centered in the roundabout driveway and positioned my car directly in front of the valet. The country club was vast and included a golf course and open prairie for horseback riding.

The on-staff valet opened our doors and escorted us out of the car.

"Good evening, ma'am. Shall we park your car for the evening or pull up for a few hours?" The valet asked.

"I'll only be an hour or so." I was confident.

"Sounds good. Your vehicle is in good hands," he reassured me.

As my car pulled off, Asya and I stood outside the traditional grand steps that lead up to the door.

"How are we getting in?" Asya asked.

"Why we're prestigious guest of Catherine Winsdale of course, my dear." I pulled out my high-end bougie vernacular.

"Well, pip-pip and cheerio mothafucka."

We were consumed by the extravagant interior design of the inside of the club that we almost didn't notice the hosts flagging us down.

"Hi there. Can I help direct you to your party?" she asked

"Yes. Of course. We're guests of Catherine Winsdale."

"Oh, for the wine club. Of course. Follow me." She escorted us. "You must be new to the club. I can't say I've met your acquaintance before."

"You could say we're new. Taya Roberts," I introduced myself.

"A pleasure." She accepted my greeting and then turned to Asya.

"Oh. I'm Asya. I've been here several times

before. I'm surprised we haven't met," she lied.

"Really? Me too. My apologies for not recognizing you. I try to make friends with all of our members.

I shot a sharp look at Asya. She smiled. I could read her mind. She's thinking, "If I have to be here I might as well have a little fun."

We reached the group that gathered around a large table in the back foyer area accompanied by more than you average amount of wine. I scoped the scene quickly: all women, one Latina chick, and everybody else was white.

"Mrs. Winsdale, your guests." The hostess completed her job.

I immediately jumped in as Catherine stood from her seating looking incredibly surprised. "So funny thing, I received an invite for your wine club from a friend on Facebook…" I looked around the room in a fake attempt to find my imaginary friend. "…doesn't look like she's here… and I immediately recognized the name Catherine Winsdale of Wilson and Winsdale PR. We have a formal meeting scheduled for next week. I'm Taya Roberts. Pleasure to meet you."

My approach was to hit her with way too much information so she couldn't check me on all the topics. Obviously, I wasn't invited by a friend nor was I internet stalking her but those were facts for Asya and me.

"Well hello there, Mrs. Roberts." She shook my

hand.

"All my friends call me Taya. Feel free. Oh, and where are my manners, this is Asya Young, my esteemed business partner." I pointed to Asya.

Asya properly adjusted her suit jacket as a power move gesture to show confidence and then introduced herself. "Such a pleasure to have the opportunity to meet you, Mrs. Winsdale. That Microsoft public deal you closed last year is still my favorite article write up to date." Catherine embraced Aysa's handshake.

"Well that was one for the books let me tell you!" She laughed. "Ladies, join us please. There is plenty of wine to go around."

We nailed it. This is what I like to call kissing ass with a purpose. We took our seats. I was right next to Catherine while Asya sat on the opposite side of the table. We properly introduced ourselves to the entire table and quickly became the life of the event. We easily had the most entertaining personalities of all eight people at the table and everyone knew it. Our new acquaintances wanted to know everything about us: where we went to school, what we studied, what are we doing professionally, what motivated us to move from Texas to Florida, and so forth and so on. All topics that we wanted to discuss anyway.

"So, Asya and I decided to make the big leap from Corporate America to startups. We come with a litany of professional experience and knew with a little bit of effort we could make it work," I added to the conversation.

"Well you two must meet more people. Being

new in this area cannot be helping the growth of your business. How about this? We have a meeting next week, right?" Catherine looked over at me.

"Sure do, Tuesday morning."

"I'll have my admin add a line item for me to align you with some of my good friends who have similar interests. Oh and we must get you a write up in the *Tech Tribune*, it's the best way to showcase your new entrepreneurial endeavors." At this point, Catherine was an entire bottle of wine in so she was rambling a little.

"Just to make things easier, I'll send a note out tonight as a reminder. I think all of these ideas are great," I sealed the deal.

"Yes, Taya I love your ambition. Your forward approach will take you very far in this business." She had no idea.

Just as we predicted, we only needed an hour or so. Asya and I finished our last sip of wine and then made personal goodbyes to all the ladies at the table. Then we made our way to the front door.

"Bitchhhhhh," Asya slid out under her breath as we walked away.

"Can you say, secure the bag?" I followed. We both laughed.

"After all that wine, I gotta pee. I'll meet you in the front," Asya said as she ran off to the restroom.

"Cool."

I stood outside in front of the country club checking the time. It was getting late, a little after ten.

As I waited for my car to pull up I noticed two tall brothers in tailored suits walking up the stairs to the entrance. Both of them stared me down like two cheetahs checking out a zebra at a waterhole. The one on the left: dark skinned, low cut, black suit. The one on the right: brown skin tone, sponge brushed low fro, clean line up, full beard, blue suit. Both snacks. They stopped once they got to me.

"Say, bro, how long have we been members here? And we never seen a sister this fine."

"Never even seen a sister in here period" His friend followed.

"That's unfortunate for both of y'all," I interjected the conversation.

"Brandon McArthur, attorney at law. This is my boy, Todd," the fine brother in blue introduced himself.

"Todd Jefferson Jr., M.D.," the brother in black stated.

At this point, Asya was approaching and my car was pulling up.

"Taya, not superficial enough to introduce myself by my profession, Roberts. Nice to meet you both." I pointed to my Tesla. "Unfortunately, I have to apologize for cutting this conversation short, my car is here." Asya glanced over the two men in front of me then looked over in confusion as to why I was blowing them off but she didn't say much.

"No need to apologize, Miss Roberts. I know you got a business card on you. Let me get that. Never hurts to add a new face to your network." Brandon was smooth.

I pulled a business card from my gold carrying case. "Agreed, can never have too many connections. A pleasure meeting you both." Then, I flagged Asya to follow me to the car. Brandon and Todd watched our exit and then went inside the club.

"Taya what the fuck did I miss?" Asya asked once we were in the car.

"You didn't miss nothing."

"Why did you curve that fine ass man? I'm confused."

"Hello I'm in a relationship, Asya."

"But are you married? Because last I recall we're not ready to take men too seriously this year."

She had a point. "I feel it but regardless I had to curve him initially. Men love the chase."

"True."

5

CHESS MOVES

I woke up to the sound of Asya moaning in pleasure from her bedroom. Apparently, getting some head from the words I could make out. Never mind the fact that I had no clue she even had a dick appointment, but whoever this man is seriously talented. This must be the universe's way of telling me I need to get up and move around.

A long hot shower, a good scalp scrub and blow dry later and I was feeling brand new. I had plenty of work to do. Now, with this new Winsdale relationship, I knew I needed to get our company PR ready. If all goes right, we'll be busy with press work for the next couple of weeks. I walked into the kitchen with my bath towel wrapped around my body and freshly blown out hair all over my head. I opened the refrigerator and grabbed the half empty bottle of orange juice and a bowl of strawberries.

"Asya, can Mimosa Friday be a thing?!" I yelled while still inside the fridge. I peeked over the top of the door only to be startled by a visitor in our house.

"Oh shit!" I jumped.

"My bad. I didn't mean to scare you." It was Asya's early booty call guest. He looked strangely familiar.

"Yea well you did." I rolled my eyes. "I guess since you're here, would you like a mimosa?"

"Nah, Taya, I'm straight. I try not to drink this early."

"Do I know you?" I followed as I shuffled through the kitchen cabinets looking for champagne.

"Damn you don't remember me?" He answered my question with a question.

"If I remembered I wouldn't ask." I glanced over at him and his bare chest.

"Todd. Me and my boy met you outside the country club last week."

"Ohhh yea. I knew you looked familiar."

I found the champagne.

"I'm surprised you do, the way you curved my boy that day. I'm shocked you remember anything about us," he laughed.

"I did not curve. I was busy at the time."

"Yea alright."

Asya joined us just as I started pouring my drink. She was in a matching bra and panty set with her titties setting on her chin.

"Oh, we making mimosas? Let me get one."

"My typa bitch," I cosigned and poured two glasses.

"When were you going to tell me you pulled, Swole Doctor over there?" I pointed to Todd who was sitting on our couch flipping through channels.

"First of all, Mr. Swole is fine," she started.

"He's alright." I glanced over.

"Secondly, he found me. Followed up with that nosey ass receptionist from the club, got my name, and found me on Facebook."

"So, he's a doctor and a stalker. Nice," I said sarcastically.

"Or he just saw a fine chocolate bitch that he needed to taste." Asya stuck her tongue out before she sipped her drink.

"Yea, I see this fine chocolate bitch was getting licked like a spoonful of peanut butter this morning. I can't hate on that." We laughed.

"Anyway, I'm about to get dressed and go to work. I have so much shit to do for these press releases. Plus, we need a motherfucking building ASAP." I ran down my agenda.

"Yea I'ma get rid of dude then finish working through these hires for our engineering staff. And, yes, a building would be great. I can't hire people and tell them to work from Starbucks."

"Say no more. I'm on it." I grabbed my drink and the strawberries and headed for my room to get dressed for the day. "Nice seeing you, Todd." I waved as I disappeared down the hall.

I talked to Rashad on the phone as I got dressed. He was sitting in traffic on his way to work. Rashad was more like my best friend than a boyfriend. I gossiped with him about the dude Asya brought in, he said I sounded jealous. I was, lowkey. We talked about our game plans for the day and shared advice. And he helped me pick out my fit for the day. I ended up wearing fitted high waisted skinny jeans, a tucked in white cami, nude closed toe suede pumps, and freshly flat ironed hair.

•••

The city was moving today.

There was at least two hundred million things I needed to accomplish but I was focused on two specifically: getting my bands up and my money. Same things but two different angles.

"Hi... yes, my name is Taya Roberts I'm looking for Brandon McArthur... Oh great he's available? I need a quick thirty minutes with him if you could add me to his calendar... Perfect, oh and no need to give him a heads up, he's expecting me," I bold faced lied.

"Thank you," I offered his assistant in my most likable tone.

I had a plan. And I was curious about what Brandon had on his mind when he handed me his card. All beneficial to my two goals for the day.

My bag was the focal point of my fit for the day. These jeans and nude tones got me looking basic but my seven thousand dollar bag got me looking like a rich bitch who's just chillin. The power of an expensive handbag is real; plus, I was carrying my whole office in this thing: MacBook, sketch designs, tablet for demos, both my cell phones, and my flask.

"Miss Roberts, you can see Mr. McArthur in his office."

"Thank you." I passed her to enter the wooden double door entrance to his office.

He looked down at his notebook as I walked in. I quietly closed the door behind me and gathered myself as I walked toward his desk. His office was large with a corner view. He was a big deal to his firm and I could tell just from looking at his office.

He looked up.

"Wow." He was shocked. I flashed my pretty white teeth in his direction as I watched his pleasant surprise set in.

"Good morning." I was soft and polite as I took a seat in front of his desk.

"Definitely a good morning. To what do I owe this pleasure? I'm curious." He finally came up for air and started using his brain as he reared back in his desk chair and folded his arms.

I pulled out my tablet, opened it to a pitch deck, and slid the tablet across his desk.

"I didn't get a chance to properly introduce myself at the country club—"

"You had the chance you just didn't want to," he cut me off.

I jumped back in. "I have a completely different

opinion about that but that's a conversation for another day, the point here being that I think we can do some great business together."

He leaned back in. "What kind of business?"

"Do you want a new client?" I asked point blank

"I only deal with high profile portfolios," he tried me.

I pointed at the tablet. "Check me out. I'm as high profile as a sole proprietor can get and, not to mention, LLC with my business partner, Asya. Check out our bottom line, we're legit. I'm foreseeing some heavy legality issues coming into scope soon for us and what's better than getting a Black man to partner with us?"

He raised his eyebrow. "My firm can cover you. But the real question is: why did you come to me directly? With a portfolio like this any law firm in the city would bend over backwards to onboard you."

I smiled. "Yes of course I could work with any firm but I'm expecting a personalized experience. I was hoping you could provide that for me?" I was flirtatious but definitely speaking facts about my business.

"If you let me take you out, I'll provide a personal experience."

"Take me out? A date?" I clarified.

"A date," he confirmed.

I thought about it for a second. *He really thinks this is ok? Trading dates for business. Men.*

"We can do brunch. A date is a little too much for me right now but I could enjoy endless mimosas with you." I couldn't let him get it all on the first try.

He nodded. "That's fair. Brunch it is."

•••

After I wrapped up what I would later consider the most cost effective legal partnership, I made it my job to close my physical location problem. Catherine and her affluent inner circle opened all the right doors for me. I hadn't even had my official formal meeting with Catherine, but since she posted our group picture from Wine-Wednesday on social media and tagged the business, our stock has been on the rise. It was up to me now to make the right connections.

With my new found information I did exactly what my business media marketing professor taught as the very first rule of marketing: connect. I spent the entire rest of my day doing drive-bys with people I knew that worked with City Hall on zoning, permissions, localization laws, and everything under that. By 6 p.m., all I needed was Catherine to sign off on a contract to allow our business to occupy a space in her division. Next Tuesday was the day.

6

PULLOUT

There was literally nothing more satisfying than getting strong stroked by a man that was infatuated with your appearance. Rashad was a fiend for my body; not one single part of my body was he not willing to glide his tongue across and taste. With both my thighs firmly tucked under his arms, he effortlessly slid in and out of me, covering his entire dick with sticky glaze every time he contracted. Rashad is a grown man, meaning his manhood was mature. And with that came great responsibility, he made sure he took care of my body every time we were physical because he knew how easy it was for him to make the wrong move and rip me to pieces.

His favorite part of having sex with me, like any other man, was each and every one of my soft parts. My thighs, titties, and, ranked most favorable, my ass. He had one of my knees on the counter and the other leg in his hand as he stroked me from the back but then he stopped out of nowhere. He pulled out. For the first time within the last fifteen minutes, I took a breath. I turned to face him. His head hung low as he took his first few real breaths as well.

"What's wrong?" Never have I ever had a nigga pull his raw dick out before busting, not on purpose anyway.

"That shit is wet as fuck," he answered. I nodded.

"Yea. You're welcome. So what's wrong?" I asked the question again. I was genuinely confused.

"This is the best pussy I've ever had."

At this point, I was drying out so I grabbed his shirt off the floor, threw it on, and walked toward the bathroom to get the drip off my inner thigh. "And you're just now having this grand epiphany whilst we fuck… today … just now?" I was searching. He trailed me to the bathroom.

"Nah, I been knew…" He stood in the doorway with his head resting on the threshold, remaining vague as hell. He looked fine, as usual, but he was saying so much less.

I turned my back to the sink that I just used to get a quick hoe-bath in. "Rashad. What's up?" He stood there naked, dick still very long and having a hard time retracting it's erection. An erection I was one thousand percent prepared to handle, by the way.

"I fucked this chick at my job… a week ago," he

48

blurted.

My face went from concerned, to blank, and, then, immediately into pissed.

"You did what? You say you fuck with some chick at your job? As in she's cool. Y'all are having great conversations cool. OR…" My voice grew a few decibels. "…did you say y'all fucked?!" I punched his chest.

"An accident, Taya. I swear to God." He was finally using completely whole sentences.

"Excuse me. How do you manage to accidentally fit that long dick into anything let alone a vagina that I'm sure you had to undress? Unless bitches at your job walking around in coochie-less slacks. Which would explain this story a little bit better than you're explaining right now." I was in my mothafuckin bag with the questions.

"An accident, as in I wasn't intending for it to get that deep." He was trying to explain himself.

I walked past him, through the hallway of his apartment back into the kitchen.   "Intending?" I wanted to make sure I was hearing everything clearly. "As in you had intentions for this person? As in you had enough time to think about this person's position in your life. Enough time that you had a game plan as to how you wanted the relationship to evolve? Accident you say?" Again, in my bag.

"Taya. Don't do that. You know what the fuck I'm saying. Shorty was in my face for a little bit but I was never planning on fucking her."

"Well… looks like that plan backfired." I was collecting my actual clothes that were scattered across his living room in efforts to gather myself so that I could go and cry in my car.

"I fucked up. You know I'm not that kind of nigga."

"Except you're exactly that kind of nigga. And to think I've been curving men because I thought I finally bagged a good one." I laughed but I was sad as hell.

Rashad found his sweats and covered up his nude lower half as I moved furiously to put my outfit back together. The one day I had on a complicated layered look is the same day a bitch needed to get dressed fast enough to escape her problems.

"You know I'm not that kind of nigga, Taya. I wouldn't have told you if I was. I can't lie to you and I've felt bad ever since it happened last week. I wanted to be honest with you."

"Now what? Now that you've been honest."

"We grow." He dropped some cliché ass line that he probably saw on one of them bogus episodes of *Catfish*.

I laughed. "Yea right." I was finally fully clothed. Back to looking like a bad bitch with business. I packed my handbag with my phone and grabbed my keys.

"I'll tell you what happens. You can get the fuck on. I'm literally too fucking busy for this shit right now and you know that. But, I appreciate you not continuing to waste my life any further." I opened his front door and made sure that thing was firmly shut behind me. Then, I left in my Tesla, blazing a hundred on the highway.

7

THE CABINETS ARE FINE

"Um, Taya…" Asya asked as I slammed through our cabinets looking for a bottle of Champagne.

"Yea?" I didn't look up.

"Looking for something?" She was trying to be helpful.

"Where's the fucking Champagne?"

"We drank it all, over mimosas. Remember?"

I did remember. "Ok, then, where's the hard liquor?"

She pointed. "There's some Cognac in the top cabinet above the refrigerator."

I opened the cabinet, grabbed the bottle of Hennessy and took a shot directly from the bottle. Then, I poured a strong amount into a glass and sat down at our island.

"Should I be concerned?" Asya took the bottle and poured a small shot for herself. "What happened today?"

It was late. A little after 11 p.m. Our floor-to-ceiling bay window drapes were pulled back and we could see the lake glisten as the moonlight lit it up.

"We have all our city permits submitted. And Catherine connected me with some people that helped make that process super fast. We also have sufficient legal coverage just in case anything goes left. Oh… and Rashad and I are finished." I swallowed the remains of my drink.

Asya took her shot after I spilled what was upsetting me. "Let me guess… he cheated?"

"You should audition for *Jeopardy*. We'll need the money later." I was making dark jokes, trying to not drown in my own self-pity.

"I really wish I could say I'm surprised. But… you know they all cheat right" She looked over at me, I glared. "Not that that excuses anything…" She made it clear she wasn't defending anything.

"Yea… I did know. That doesn't change that it hurts every time." I poured more.

Asya rested her head on my shoulder, saying nothing. She's the kind of person that doesn't try to make things feel better or look for the bright side. She's real. We sat on the island in silence finishing the bottle until we could barely hold our heads up straight and then we retreated to our respective parts of the house.

•••

"Who hired you? Because you're literally making zero sense right now."

I was on a call with an overseas agent who was doing a piss poor job of representing one of our suppliers for our hardware equipment.

"Look, Mister whatever-in-the-fuck your name is, I need to track a shipment that should have been delivered weeks ago. I feel like that's probably the core description of your job because when I called and selected two to be routed to a person who could help me track a shipment … Well, what exactly do you know? You're useless. I hope this call is being recorded. Whoever is listening this rep couldn't find a nickel in cash register. Do better." I hung up with an attitude.

I was working from home, taking calls and trying to handle business.

"Taya can you not take your frustrations out on these very innocent customer service reps? That's the third person you've compared to a nickel today." Asya was working from home too.

"A bitch is angry. What can I say?"

"You should get out the house. For the sake of our cabinets, the missing liquor, and any poor soul that has to encounter you via a phone call." She never looked up from her laptop.

"The cabinets are fine," was my only response. Then, the doorbell rang. Per usual, Asya didn't even budge. It's like she hears a doorbell and automatically assumes it's not for her.

"Oh, don't worry, allow me." My sarcasm paired well with my attitude.

Asya was not even attempting to give a fuck.

I cracked the door open just enough to see who it was. It was Callum, our neighbor. The handy one who helped us get our drapes up.

"Good morning." It was not a good morning but whatever.

"Hi, Taya. Nice to see you." He was polite.

I smiled. "Is there something I can help you with?" I slide to the side to allow him to enter the foyer. Asya waved from the couch.

"No, not really. I was actually about to catch a jog around the lake, you know since it's such a nice day, and was wondering if you ladies wanted to join?"

I rubbed the back of my head, looking for an excuse.

Asya jumped in. "I'm actually crazy busy right now but it's funny because Taya was just telling me how she needed to get out the house and clear her mind. Doesn't a nice jog sound fun, Taya?" I shot her the strongest look. My forehead was so tight.

"Yea, I'd love to get it in with you, Taya. I'll try to keep up," Callum joked.

A jog did actually seem like a good idea. "Let me change really quick." I disappeared off into my room to change into a workout fit. Black leggings and a black sports bra to match my dark mood.

Callum and I jogged around and over the lake

three times before he called a quits. I've made this jog quite a few times since moving in; it's such a serene, quiet space plus it helps keep this body on point.

"I basically uprooted my Florida life to move here with him. We only been dating close to a year but I thought he was going to be the one," I explained my situation.

"I get that. And, again, I'm sorry it happened to you but you gotta know that these types of things are not a reflection of you in any kind of way."

"Are you sure? Because at some point I need to take responsibility for picking these shitty ass men. I didn't even tell you about my last ex from Florida." I briefly thought about Money Mike.

We stopped running and grabbed a bench near the water. "Look… a part of that is a reflection of what you like but a large part of it is based on the person and where they are in their life. It's not like people walk around with a sign listing all their baggage, flaws, and insecurities. I've only known you for a few months, Taya but you're a risk taker. You gamble on things that could have a high reward and you also know that sometimes those risks come with losses."

"Ok, yea but losing a couple thousand when I make a bad investment feels easier than making a poor choice on a man. I can always get my money back but how am I going to go back and collect my pussy?"

He died laughing. "You don't gotta worry about that. You're still a hot commodity out here. You don't need that pussy back, consider it a donation." Now, I was laughing.

"Well, I'm so over donating. You wanna head back?"

I worked nonstop that night. My to-do list was empty by the time 3 a.m. hit and so were two bottles of Cabernet Sauvignon. I was locked in, knocking everything out. A part of me wanted to just hide in my room and the other more powerful side of me was hungry. I had shit to do and it definitely didn't involve me feeling sorry for myself.

8

BRUNCH, AS PROMISED

"Tell me something about you that I don't know," he was trying to mind fuck me. Or get to know me. Borderline both.

"Before I was a startup entrepreneur, I was a marketing tycoon." I took a strategic sip of my cocktail to draw attention to my matte red lip.

"Why am I not surprised? Marketing suits you."

"And how would you even know that?" Our conversation was light, friendly, and flirty.

"The way you slid into my office unannounced and pitched an idea that I didn't even hesitate to agree to. Corporate perseverance written all over you."

I took Brandon up on his date proposition, well, brunch after I rebranded his idea. I had already agreed to it and, plus, now I needed an excuse to be entertained.

"Tell me more." I folded my arms and crossed my legs as a gesture to signal my interest in the topic.

"Nothing more to tell. Your demeanor is the single most attractive thing about you. It's always about the style for me. When I first saw you a few weeks back, you were just standing outside of the country club, but there was something particularly graceful about the way that you were waiting that caught my attention. You never come off rushed or ungathered. Tailored. Dressed well. Scented for pleasure. You being gorgeous is just icing on this cake." He leaned over the table, grabbing my index finger to pull my hand close to his face and gently placed his lips across the back of my hand. A chill sprawled up my spine but I didn't move or break eye contact.

I retracted my hand, sitting forward in my seat and grabbed my glass. "Flattered. And impressed with your attention. Most of those attributes come off more subtly, glad to see you paying attention." I couldn't bring myself to simply accept him compliments.

He smiled.

Brandon McArthur. Jesus. Nothing short of high quality, fantasy-like, in high demand Black man. I was always into rich men. My background included NBA, NFL, Wall Street, and PhDs. But, in my prime, money and looks were enough. I got a little older and the list of shit I found myself attracted to became more refined. Types of income became important, his accessibility to me started to creep higher on the list, his ability to hold an interesting conversation was a must; and, unlike in the past, he could absolutely not be involved in a relationship. That includes baby mamas and "we're just talking."

"Your turn. Tell me something about you that I don't know."

"I used to be married," he responded. I was not expecting that one.

"Divorced? Or separated?" I needed him to clarify.

"Divorced almost five years now. Just thought I'd get that one out before you thought I was trying to hide something from you."

"Why... did you get divorced?" I was interested to see if he would share.

"We wasn't feeling it no more. We got married young, while I was in undergrad. I studied a lot while working on my masters and law degree. She always felt like an afterthought."

"Was she?"

"An afterthought?" I nodded. "You know. Not at first, she wasn't. I was into her, in love. But after we started going through the trenches, she started losing focus on what we both agreed to be our goals. I was getting my law degree and she was pursuing vet school. That bonded us in the beginning. She started complaining about my study hours after she didn't even attempt to enter a veterinarian program after her undergrad degree. So, I guess so. She became less relevant to me because we didn't share any life goals anymore."

"Wow." I was blown away by his transparency.

"You ever been married?"

"Never. Never been engaged either."

"Cause you declined all the offers." He didn't even ask. He knew the answer.

I laughed. Just a little. "So what's your relationship—"

"Single, as hell," he answered before I could finish the question. "What about you?"

"Same."

It was barely two hours later before I was getting slayed in-between Brandon's sheets like a dragon. It was ice cold in his high-rise, all slate grey decorated apartment. His king-sized bed engulfed my body as he drilled me into the center of his mattress.

Covers enveloped both of our bodies leaving just our heads and shoulders exposed. *Fuck.* He softly let out occasionally as he wasted no time getting to work. Other than that, all you could hear was our skin clapping together and my erotic moans. I was enjoying getting piped down royally. After he decided he couldn't bear the tension of watching my titties bounce in his face, he turned me over onto my stomach, gripped his hands around my waist, and stroked me with my legs closed. I palmed his black throw pillows as I searched for a space to grip. He was tagging my insides. Steady, fast-paced power strokes. With tenacity, Brandon hiked my waist in the air placing my cheeks against his abs. By now, his soft "fucks" were full blown moans. He gripped the meat on my booty until it oozed past his fingers then followed the motions with loud slaps, forcing my ass to bounce. He never broke the stroke. Gripped, slapped, fucked were on repeat. He grabbed my right thigh and aggressively flipped me onto my back. I caught my breath.

"Let me get them lips though." He spoke an actual sentence. I thought he meant he wanted head but he actually wanted to kiss.

He leaned in kissing and sucking on my neck as he assumed his position sliding his dick perfectly back inside. Before I knew it we were passionately intertwining our lips together with the occasional tongue while he stroked me holding both my thighs under his arms. His lips were soft and the kisses were sensual. The best part about kissing while we fucked was that he still moaned in between. I heard everything he was saying.

Before he knew it he was drowning in my pussy. So much so that he was saying my name on repeat as he filled the condom. And, just like that, he was hooked.

I laid in his bed facing the ceiling. He laid on his stomach cradling a pillow with both his cut up biceps exposed.

"I really hope that was as good for you as it was for me." He didn't even open his eyes. His words were even muffled because his face was mostly inside the pillow.

"I enjoyed every second." I was honest.

"Good. Cause that's about to be happening a lot. Like a lot, a lot."

I smiled because I already knew that was coming but then I just let it flow and fell asleep in his plush bed.

9

FUCKING: A TIMELESS PASTIME

"What happened to not coming off too strong? and making them wait? The chase, remember?" Asya reminded me why I don't tell her shit.

"Ok, but did you hear me when I said the man stroked me to sleep?"

"Mmm-hmm, I heard you. I also see love didn't bring yo ass home last night," she joked.

I laughed. "Hey, it be like that."

"No, ma'am, it don't be like that for normal ass people. Everybody not getting casually cuffed by a fine ass fit lawyer."

"Asya you're fucking a doctor, spare me this normal people spiel."

"That's pure coincidence and, honestly, I

wouldn't even be getting piped by this doctor if you didn't completely get the attention of his best friend. So again us normal people can't relate," Asya countered.

I rolled my eyes.

"Also, can I just call out that you're reverting to old Taya? Or is it too soon?"

"I knew that was coming. I'm not reverting. Old me would bag the nigga at the strip club blowing all his bands on strippers and bottles."

"So, new-hoe-you only getting sheet slayed by prestigious money throwers? A sophisticated hoe," Asya continued.

"I resent that. I was always a sophisticated bougie type hoe. Don't play me."

She laughed. "Ok, but do me a favor and don't lose focus of our business."

"I'm offended you even feel like you need to say that. I'm focused."

"Good. And second favor: call Rashad back. This mothafucka has called my phone one too many times and I know he's not trying to contact me."

I didn't even know Rashad was looking for me. I blocked him the night he told me he cheated. "Block him. Cause I'm most def not calling his ass." I deaded the conversation.

"Copy." She didn't even try to dig deeper.

It took me all of six and a half hours to realize that I wasn't nearly as into Brandon as he was into me. He called me this morning after I left his house to make sure I made it home safely. Then, he texted me twice calling me *gorgeous* and *beautiful* or whatever. Honestly, the pussy couldn't have been that good. Then again... *of course it was.*

Regardless of everything that happened to me in the past week or so, one thing has remained the same: I needed to land, without a single snag, my Catherine Winsdale pitch on Tuesday. I needed her to sign the third party contract and secure our space in the new tech hub of Austin. It was that our business to be in this space. Plus, Asya completed her engineer pipeline and we had a team ready to start in a few weeks. The pressure was on.

"Ok, but tell me what you want to accomplish in this meeting?" Callum asked. I invited him over to listen to my pitch for Winsdale.

"Callum. Not sure if you've been listening but I need her to sign this contract." I was getting spicy at this point. Plus the margaritas Asya was whipping up in the blinder were not helping.

"I get that. But your whole pitch is so... You centric . What's in it for her?" He was cozy on our couch as he critiqued my presentation.

He was right. I was taking this from the wrong angle. I sat on the couch across from him with the most intense look on my face as I thought through what he was saying.

"Not that your pitch isn't good—"

"You ain't even gotta lie, Callum," Asya cut him off from the kitchen.

"No, I'm not lying. I'm just saying, it's a business deal. You gotta be more well-rounded. And, if you're not going to do that at least take it from her perspective first. Taya, you know marketing."

"No, you're right." He was. I do know marketing. I had work to do.

"Ok, but enough about this let's switch the subject and more margaritas please." I looked over toward the kitchen.

"Yea, Callum, tell us something interesting. What's your favorite hobbies? What kind of women are you into? Who you fucking?" Asya asked, smirking behind the bottle of tequila.

He blinked in shock but then quickly remembered where he was and how blunt our conversations get in this house. Then, he gathered himself in preparation for a response. I was actually curious about who he was fucking too. He's not a bad looking guy.

"Well, my hobbies—" he started but Asya cut him off.

"To be clear, that hobby question was a warm-up. You like fixing things and working out, blah. Now tell us about your sex life." Asya was crazy straightforward as she delivered freshly whipped up margaritas to the two of us.

Callum laughed so hard. "Um... ok. I'll pretend like this isn't an extremely personal question," he started. I made myself comfortable on the couch, crossing my legs and sitting up straight.

"I'm not fucking anyone, as you'd say. I'd also

never describe sex with someone I care about like that. But, just matching your tone. I'm single. The last time I was in a relationship was a few years ago."

"So… you don't fuck?" I asked him more specifically.

"I guess I do. I just don't call it that."

"Nah you would know if you're fucking. Fucking is a different kind of sex. It's the kind that is one hundred percent only about you and getting off." I made sure to clarify. Asya joined us in the living room, nodding in agreement.

"Oh, well then, no. I don't fuck."

"Every time you have sex, you're into the other person?" Asya wanted him to elaborate.

"Every person I've had sex with I was interested in beyond physical appearance. Women that I wanted to invest in emotionally."

"Even when you were in college?" I kind of didn't believe him.

"I had one girlfriend the whole time I was in college. So yea."

"And you didn't cheat?" Asya added.

"Not once."

"Ok, but have you ever cheated?" I thought about Rashad.

"I haven't ever really seen the point of that."

"I cheated once," Asya jumped in.

"Once?" I didn't believe her.

"Yes. Once. Why you gotta say it like that?

Anyway, I cheated on this guy I was dating a while back in Florida because he did not eat pussy. And anybody that knows me, knows I need to have my pussy licked like a popsicle."

"She's not lying," I corroborated her story.

"So, I let this fine ass man in my advanced computer science course swirl my clit in the parking lot one day. Got caught by my boyfriend's friend and that was the end of the relationship. So now, I refuse to take anybody seriously that says they don't eat."

"Wow." Callum was shocked. I wasn't. I heard that story many times.

"I think it's important to know what you don't like just as much as you know what you do like," I added.

"Why didn't you figure that out before you got into a relationship with him?" Callum asked curiously.

"I didn't know I needed to ask or know how much I required head."

"I see. That's tough but I personally couldn't bear the weight of cheating on a person I love. Call me lame or whatever but that's not my style." Callum was into the conversation at this point.

His mind was stimulating. Even though a part of me thought that what he was saying was bullshit the other part of me wanted him to be telling the truth. Just to give us a glimpse of hope.

"Taya, call me back. It's Brandon." I let my voicemails play through my car speakers. I really would have never guessed Brandon to be this pressed; he's

70

high quality but his thirstiness was killing his brand. He was so smooth and well put together at first and, now, to see him insecurely trying to solidify our connection less than twenty-four hours after our first sexual encounter, is just –well– quite frankly unattractive. But then I thought about it. *Since when is it a bad thing to have a man take you seriously after you gave him some ass?* So, I called him back.

"Hey… yea, I know. I was super busy today trying to get things together," I lied. I was drinking tequila.

"Yea… last night was definitely a good time." I let him say whatever he needed to get off his chest. "Tonight? I can't still gonna be pretty busy… yea I can make this weekend work. Oh, I love Italian." I do and I really don't know how he knows that. "Ok sounds good… yea… ok… bye." Then, I hung up.

Just my luck. Now, I gotta go on another date with this clingy fool. The only bright side is that dating will keep my mind off of Rashad; hopefully not at the expense of my sanity.

10

GAME TIME

"Taya LaMonica-Rochelle Roberts, you gone drive me crazy if you practice this damn presentation one more time. I swear to you it's perfect. Now shut thee fuck up… and I mean that in the sincerest way possible," Asya shouted.

"First off, who is LaMonica-Rochelle? Why I gotta have that long ass fake middle name! Secondly, bitch, this is for both of us! I need these words to roll seamlessly off my tongue and onto Winsdale's earlobes so that they will guide her hand to sign our contract. May a bitch practice with less scrutiny from her business partner? Damnnnn," I stated dramatically.

"Actually, no, a bitch may not because said bitch is getting on bitch number two's nerves. Again, as I recall a famous quote, 'Shut Cho Ass Up.' Thank you." Honestly, I was in tears by the end of this conversation so much so that I forgot I was about to embark on the biggest business deal of this new journey.

Asya was right, I had practiced this presentation enough times that even I was getting on my own nerves. I replayed my intro over and over again: *As the tech industry playground expands, so do partnerships. Our partnership is sure to be a longevous one…* I wondered if she'd go for that approach. I decided I'd hit her with my opening paragraph, gauge her reaction, and then pivot. If she wasn't feeling it I would hit her with the: *Okay, I'ma keep it a buck with you. I need this and I'm pretty sure I can put some bread in your pockets along the way.* I only had two approaches The Barack Obama Prestigious Approach or Katt Williams Get It How You Live Angle.

After breakfast with Asya and Todd – yes, Todd was at our house regularly – I hunted through my closet for a very specific pant suit. Had to go with the pantsuit over the skirt suit because I was doing business with a woman. Had it been a man I would wear a skirt. The game is the game. I ran across a dark navy blue fitted pant suit in the corner of my closet; since leaving my corporate marketing gig, I barely even touch suits except for occasions like these. I shook the dust off the jacket as I checked to see if it had been dry cleaned and pressed properly; did the same for the pants. I went with the all-white woven button-down Ralph Lauren collar shirt to officially seal the deal on my professional fit. Finished with diamond studs, a classic gold women's Rolex, and a dab of Chanel for the scent. I gave myself that long stare in the full body mirror and had to remind myself why I stopped wearing professional attire in the first place. I look good as shit.

"Damn," Todd reacted when I joined them in the kitchen.

"Yes. That is the correct reaction." I was feeling myself.

"If your presentation don't fuck em up them pants hugging that booty will, for sure," Asya added.

"Too tight? I don't want this middle-aged white woman to get jealous." I was curious about what she thought.

"Them pants could be two sizes too big and we'd still see that ass. Plus, Winsdale already saw your body at the country club and she didn't seem to have a problem with it then," Asya shrugged.

"You right about that." I grabbed a to-go coffee in my favorite portable FAMU mug, picked up my bag that was securely holding my laptop, tablet, and wallet, and headed for the garage. "Y'all wish me luck." I bid my farewell.

The city was a little more chill than it normal. Or it could have just been my nerves fucking with my mental. Either way, I knew it was game time. I had my power suit on, my presentation was crispy, and I had two whole cups of coffee flowing through my body.

"I'll alert Mrs. Winsdale of your arrival, Miss Roberts. One moment." Catherine Winsdale's assistant guided me to a plush loveseat in the waiting area adjacent to her office.

The whole office was littered with fine French

art. All natural colors. Very elegant and tasteful. Made me glad to have made the choice to wear a pantsuit and not the hoochie skirt I would normally pull out.

"She's wrapping up a phone call. She'll be out in just a sec." The young lady was what I would call corny but she made for a great professional assistant so I didn't hate on shorty.

"Taya. Such a pleasure to see you again, my dear." Catherine met me in the waiting area just outside her door with welcome arms. She reached for a handshake and I accepted, following her into her office.

"Please grab a seat and get comfortable. Looks like we have thirty minutes together. May I offer you a beverage? Perhaps a cocktail?" She was way too polite.

"Actually, I'll pass, grabbed a glass of water on the way in." I'd actually like a cocktail but I thought it was too early.

"Well hope you don't mind if I have one?" Catherine asked. Apparently, it's not too early.

"Absolutely not. Feel free." I motioned her to do her thing. Her office was mostly made of glass with the occasional gold accent. Super clean matching the aesthetics of her waiting area.

"Lovely to see you again." She sat down with her drink.

"Likewise. I knew I needed to grab time on your calendar as soon as possible. You know, As the tech industry playground expands so do partnerships. Our partnership is sure to be longevous one—" I started my pitch. Taking the limited time I had with her very seriously. But she cut me off before I could even get started.

"Taya, I know why you're here."

"You do?" I was shocked.

"Of course, You want the building permit on 7th Street. I run this city I know everything happening before it happens." She absolutely did.

I must have had the strongest look of confusion on my face because she continued to explain. "You've had a few meetings with some people on my team and they gave me the heads up you were coming for a partnership contract." She stood and began to walk, she sipped as she talked. "Look… Taya if it were anyone else I wouldn't have even accepted the meeting request but, you and Asya I like. How you both party busted into Wine Down Wednesday and grabbed my attention. And, not to mention, you have a very niche product that I'm very surprised to say I've never heard of before." S

"So you'll sign our deal?" That was an easier pitch than I thought.

"Mmm… yes and no" That didn't sound good. "I'll agree to giving you the space and the building permit but I want a seat at this table."

"What kinda seat we talking?" I turned off the code switch.

"Fifteen percent of net profit," she offered.

"Fifteen? As in one-five?" I stood up to leave.

"Do you have a better idea? You do need this space don't you?" She sipped her drink.

"Five percent." I negotiated. She was right I did need the space.

"Eight and I'll sign the contract now," she countered, as any legit great businessperson would.

"Fine but I want the real-estate lot facing the main street. Not the one in the back like my original proposal suggested."

"Deal. As long as you give my son a job. He just graduated with his bachelor's in computer science. He should be of use to you in some capacity." She slid in an additional ask.

I took a pause to think about what just happened. "Deal. I'll need to revise the contract but I can have that done tonight and shoot it over to you via email."

"Sounds perfect." She took another sip. "I knew I liked you for a reason." She smiled as she reclaimed her seat.

I really couldn't tell if I was being hustled or if I just came up. But either way, we got what we needed. "A pleasure as always. I look forward to our long-term partnership.

"Likewise." She held her glass in the air as I gathered my things for an exit.

I was experiencing mixed emotions as I exited the tall building Catherine occupied in downtown Austin when I heard a faint voice from behind me call my name.

"Taya. Hold up." I turned around to find Rashad trying to catch up to me from down the street.

I rolled my eyes and kept walking without

acknowledging him. But he ended up catching up to my brisk walk anyway.

"For real? You just gone act like you ain't hear me." He was only barely out of breath which didn't surprise me since he was always in the gym.

"I heard you." I didn't even look over at him.

"And you got my phone number on block clearly because you haven't answered the phone or responded to one single message."

"Mmm-hmm sounds about right."

"You really not gone talk to me at all?" I forgot how sincere he was.

"What do we have to talk about?" I stopped walking and finally looked up at him. He was wearing black slacks, black polo, brown dress shoes, and a matching belt. and I couldn't help but notice his freshly cut hair because he kept rubbing over his waves with his hand as he talked.

"Everything. I wanna, at least, hear how you feel right now. I know you not fucking with me and I get that but I'm not about to just drop it. I care about you. I don't know if you forgot that."

I shook my head. I didn't even need to say the thing I was thinking because he already knew.

"You wanna say I wasn't caring about you when I fucked another female." He took the words right out my mouth.

"Exactly. So remind me why we here?" He continued to follow me as I maneuvered through the streets.

He took a deep breath. "I need to apologize to you. I need to know you're ok. If we're being real, that's why I'm here. I get that you probably never wanna see me but selfishly I need to know how you are." He answered me.

"Seems like you been doing a lot of selfish shit lately." I am not an easy person to sway.

He dropped his head. "Unfortunately."

"How'd the meeting with Winsdale go? That was today right?" I forgot he knew all about that.

"It happened. Not sure how to feel about it but it happened." I was honest.

"Did you get the building?"

"Yea." We crossed the street at an intersection.

"Congratulations."

"She negotiated a percentage of the business profits in exchange and I made the deal."

"And that's why you don't know how to feel about it." He knew.

"Yea, plus, I didn't consult with Asya about it first. But I think I made the right call."

"You always do."

"Rashad. Don't do that. Don't try to butter me up like a flaky croissant. As far as I'm concerned we don't have any type of relationship. Dating or friendship." I got him back on topic.

"We can't even be friends, Taya. Even though we are actually friends? You just gone erase that part of our lives?"

"Oh, excuse me, am I supposed to completely

gloss over you rawing another female?"

He laughed a little. "I never said I hit raw."

"Well... that detail makes for a better story," I said. He laughed.

"I'm not asking you to forgive me or be my girl again or nothing like that. Can you just talk to me? Like on some real shit? Can you let me care about you?" He was so smooth.

"I'll think about it."

"That's all I can ask for. Oh and unblock my number cause we definitely still friends." He thought he was funny.

"Ok, well, you can stop following me now." He was literally following me around and I wasn't planning on going to my car immediately. I turned around and looked at him.

He threw his hands up to signal he didn't mean any harm, smiled then threw me the deuces and took his own path. I watched him for a little bit. *This smooth mothafucka.* How I allowed him to pull a drive-by on me and have a civilized conversation without beating his head in after he betrayed my trust was beyond me. Then, I quickly remembered I needed to tell Asya that I sold both our souls to the devil. Gameday turned into overtime quick.

11

PUBLIC RELATIONS
Mike

"I get that shit but I'm not about to commit to you how you want me to. I've said this too many times." I was on the phone, again, with one of my pieces.

"Ok. You say that like I'ma lose sleep if you go fuck another nigga... that's why I'm not tryna bag you in the first place."

I mighta been too real with her cause she hung up after that comment.

Most days, I didn't care about how these women felt and today was no different. I sped through the streets of Miami with my top off, big chillin. Shut It Down Records had opened up a new location in Atlanta a few months back and, before that, we signed a major artist who's ringing bells.

I staffed my team up in a way where I barely needed to be in the office; just the occasional staff meeting. Other than that, I spent my days networking, expanding the brand, and spending my bands. Plus I was running through hoes like water through a faucet. Every weekend it was a new one and by the time the following weekend rolled around, I'd smashed and left her on read a few times. Tasha, shorty who I just had one the phone, was a little different. I gave her a few rounds or so just because she was cool at first but, then, she started to get beside herself so, it's bout time I cut that off too.

I didn't have any remorse for the way I treated these women at all. After the whole incident with Taya, I haven't taken a female seriously. She really was supposed to be the one but she fucked that up.

"Mr. Keith." Taylor greeted me as soon as I stepped foot into my building. A five-story office building with two floors of studio space.

"Taylor, you've been my assistant way too long to be calling me that. Mike. Money Mike or whatever makes you feel comfortable," I demanded.

"With all due respect, Mr. Keith makes me feel comfortable." She smiled when I looked back at her with a side-eye. She was following me through the halls to the elevator.

"Whatever. So what's up?" I wanted to hear what was so important to her.

"I just got off the phone with an account executive from Wilson and something or other PR agency…" she started as she fumbled over the name.

"Who? Never heard of them." The elevator stopped on the fifth floor, we exited.

"You're going to get to know them. They run one of the largest public relations consulting firms on this side of the hemisphere. They got wind of Shut It Down Records and want to pick you up as a client."

"I don't need public relations consulting, Taylor."

I grabbed a water out the mini fridge next to her desk as I passed through to my office.

"Yea, except you absolutely do. Hear me out. I've been shopping for a PR representative for you for months now. Your company is growing like crazy but guess what's not growing?" She paused.

I shrugged. "I don't know. Humor me."

"You! You're not growing. Your business has tripled in revenue but your image is declining. Remember how you used to be that go-to guy for anything hip-hop related in the south? You're not that anymore. There's way too many other faces saturating this market. My guess is that you're not marketing yourself as a brand. Before, when the business was small, you didn't really have to. People saw Shut It Down and knew that Michael Keith was the owner. Now that your business is huge, people can't pin a face to the name. Hence your social capital decline." She was out of breath.

I took a seat at my desk. Folded my hands as I

leaned back in my chair. "And this Wilson and whoever can help me?"

"Not only can they help you, they can also elevate you. Make your brand real and take it to the next level. You could be like Diddy if you really wanted to." She was excited.

"Pshh. Puff wish he had this much sauce. But alright you sold me." She was convincing. "So now what?"

She stood up from the chair directly across from my desk. "I gotta make a few more calls and get a few contracts drafted and then we send you to Texas to meet your rep."

"Texas? They're not in Florida?" I wanted to confirm.

"No. They're in Austin. Oh, that's it. Wilson and Winsdale PR. The largest PR agency in the country. You can thank me later but for now, just be ready to get your life together." She walked toward the door. "I'm taking you and this company straight to the top." She got a little cocky as she left my office.

I sat there for a second thinking about what she said. I did lose a little of my juice as Money Mike and it was refreshing to hear it from somebody else. Taylor not only told me the real, she also dropped in solutions. *I'm never getting rid of shorty.*

12

THE COMPANY YOU KEEP
Mike

There was nothing about my life that was chill or easy-going, other than my personality. Every single day, I had an agenda, goals, and shit to get done. But, I made it my main goal to remain calm, steady, and cool through it all. I woke up this particular morning a little bit later than I normally do but made up for it with a quick shower and picking the first pair of black jeans and shirt that I saw.

I always felt kind of alone waking up in my big ass crib every morning. I don't know if it's the hardwood floor and the hollow walls that make it seem extra spacious or the fact that I was literally the only person that walked these halls day after day. That fact alone made me resent staying in my home any longer than I needed to; once I had clothes on my back, I was on my way out the door.

"Say, bro…" As soon as I got to my car, I made a phone call to my boy Dre.

"What you on? … Yea bet that … Shit well meet me out, grab some brunch, or something … Alright cool."

I met Dre at one of the most poppin brunch spots in the city. We liked pulling hoes at this particular location but we did it so often that now when we show up we see our old joints and the shit just be comedy.

Our entire conversation filled with "remember how shorty tried to fuck both of us on the same night" or "that bitch pussy trash but that head elite." We usually get a few salty looks and the occasional joint tried to make her way back in but me and Dre been hitting and quitting hoes for a decade now. That shit old.

"Bruh I'm surprised you ain't just fucked around and moved to Atlanta by now. You got that office out there. Might as well get on a completely new scene."

"I thought about it a few times but, shit, I don't know if that's what I wanna do yet." I entertained his thought.

"I don't know why not. You done ran through every hoe in this city," he laughed and shook his head.

"True enough. But I ain't focused on running through hoes no more, I had em all, bro. Fine model bitches, classy professionals, hood fine hoes, "good girls"," I said as I threw up some air quotes. "I'm off that."

"You tryna be on some family shit, Money Mike?" He laughed harder than he should have.

"Nigga what's funny bout that?" I was aggravated.

"No offense, Mike. But you not really that kinda dude. I can't even see you with a car seat in yo Benz." He laughed again. I ain't think the shit was funny.

Here I was approaching my thirtieth year of life and my closest friends can't even imagine me starting a family. Shit, to be real, I can't see it either. It's not like I've taken any female seriously in the last few years nor have I changed any of my lifestyle behaviors. For the last decade, I have been operating like a young ass twenty-one-year-old. And because I got money folks been letting me get away with this stagnant behavior. I started to look across the table at Dre a little different now.

"Say, nigga. While you laughing it ain't exactly like you got the perfect family. You on your second baby mama and it ain't no car seat in the back of yo shit either."

His facial expression changed. "Alright and? At least I can say I got kids."

"Yea, bro but you ain't taking care of them. I ain't even seen none of yo kids in the last few years. I don't think that shit count." I kept it real with his ass.

It was at that very moment that I realized I was hanging around some bum ass niggas. All my friends were either in the same exact boat as Dre or were a variation of me. I had been keeping company with ain't shit ass niggas so long that I turned into one.

"You know what, bro. I gotta make moves and get some shit done before I make this trip. You be easy." I threw some bills on the table to cover the tab and then I dabbed Dre up. He hit me with the head nod.

I left the establishment out the front door immediately back into the reality of my current situation. But it was at that moment that I decided I was gone try to be a better man. I had done everything I needed to do and way too much shit that I didn't need to do. I had nothing left to prove in my former life but, I had everything to prove to myself on what my future would be like. I honestly didn't know where to start.

My mind cycled through way too many thoughts in the moment, so much that I bumped head first into this woman approaching from the opposite direction. I finally looked up from the sidewalk that I had been fixated on for the last few minutes.

"Excuse you," she twisted her neck at me. Trying to gather her composure.

"Shit. My bad. I wasn't focused." I looked at her for the first time. She was definitely a type. Probably something like 5'7, deep brown skin, six or seven large cornrows with the baby hairs slicked back. She was definitely attractive. Nice lips, great style, and clearly outspoken.

"*My bad* is not an apology," she corrected me.

And she lucky as fuck that in the last thirty minutes I decided I was retiring my fuck boy ways

90

because old me, me earlier this morning, would have asked her who the fuck is she talking to.

"You right. You didn't deserve that. Let me formally apologize for inconveniencing you." I looked her directly in her full eyes decorated with long eyelashes.

I could feel the shift in her energy as I held her hand after she accepted my gesture. "It's fine. I apologize for being spicy with you."

I was shocked. *A woman that apologizes? What kind of mythical creature is this?*

"No. It's absolutely fine. I'm glad to be in your presence right now." Ok, I had only been reformed for the last few minutes so naturally, my game came out. But I remembered that I was approaching life in a new way. "Look I know you have somewhere to be so I won't hold you. Have a good day." I smiled and released her hand and went back to walking.

"Wait you didn't tell me your name," she asked me with my back turned to her. I stopped, laughed a little, and turned around.

"I'm Mike– Michael Keith," I corrected myself. "What about you?"

"Dana..." She paused. She knew the ball was in her court because I had already concluded the conversation so it was on her to shoot whatever shot she was about to take. I was intrigued; interested to see how she would approach this. "I'm going to give you one of my business cards. My personal number is on it.

I know we really didn't get a chance to interact but I like your energy so if you feel like it, you can hit me up."

I took her card. Her approach was really indirect but I get it because I didn't directly show her that I was interested in anything so she took the safe route. Then, I thought for a second, Money Mike would tell her to pull up at the crib later and blow her back out on the balcony but I was trying to be a different nigga.

"Let me think about it," I followed.

"Study long, study wrong," she smiled. This time, she was the one to turn around and walk away. And I watched her walk off too. She was shaped like a goddess and well fucking dressed at that. I looked down at her card; Professional Interior Decorator. I nodded my head.

13
GUCCI SUIT
Mike

I stayed in my office for the whole morning trying to knock shit out and planning for the next few months since I would be away from the headquarters. Taylor sat across from me helping me land the final A&R selections for the next signees.

"Michael you've been so focused these last few weeks. Like more focused than you usually are," she commented, never looking up from her laptop.

I stopped and thought about what she said.

"Taylor let me ask you something."

"What's up?" She closed her laptop and looked me intently in my eyes.

I hesitated a little bit. "Do you think I'm stagnant?"

"Oh, absolutely not the business is climbing–"

"No. Not the studio. I'm talking about me. My lifestyle, the kind of man that I am. Am I stagnant?"

Her demeanor changed. You could tell she was less confident about this answer. "Um... how truthful do you want me to be?"

"Brutally honest."

"Professionally, you are goals. But your personal life is kind of sad. You don't respect women, you don't value family, and you don't give back to the community. It's almost like your social life is stuck in your early 20s."

I crossed my arms and sat back in my chair. "Yea I peeped the same thing the other day."

She smiled at me from across my desk then she opened her laptop back and went to work.

"So I met this woman the other day, she gave me her business card but I have no idea how to respectfully approach somebody I wanna fuck."

She laughed. "Are you only trying to have sex with her? Because if so you need to say that or don't waste her time in general."

"Nah, I'm not tryna just fuck, I definitely do want to but she had a whole different vibe about her."

"Oh, so you liked something about her other than her body?" She clarified.

"Yea I think so."

"What was it that you liked?"

"I think I just fuck with the fact that she took a shot at me even after I acted like I wasn't interested. Something about her just came off as determined."

"Hmmm, this setup sounds very familiar."

94

"What you mean?" I didn't know what the fuck she was referring to.

"That's your type. You like attractive headstrong alpha women."

"Oh, is that what we calling it?"

"Based on your response, that's what it sounds like. So here's my follow up question. Are you willing to learn about this person without having sex with her on the first night?"

My face grew tense. I wasn't sure. "I would bust her down right now."

"Sounds like a no, Michael. Don't waste that woman's time."

"Nahhhh but I'm tryna change. So, yes, I'm trying to do this different." I attempted to bring her back into the conversation.

"Well then call her. Don't text, call. And offer to take her to a nice quiet place where both of you can learn about each other."

"A quiet place... like my house?"

"No. A place where she wouldn't think you was on no slick shit."

"I can be on some slick shit anywhere truth be told."

"Take her to Cortez the wine bar downtown. It's super cute and very lowkey. Jazz music in the background. It's a date I would die to go on."

"Can you help me book that?"

"I'm on it," she said, picking up her laptop to go

back to her desk right outside of my office. "You should make that call in the meantime."

She left and I sat there still for a moment. It had been about two weeks since I bumped into Dana but I looked at her card every day since then. Professional Interior Decorator printed on a small matte black card along with her name Dana Renee, her email address and her personal cell number. I grabbed my cell and input the Florida based phone number. I stood up and paced my office not really sure how I was about to deliver this message but confident that I could.

It rang about four times and just as I was ready to hang up a soft voice responded on the other end.

"This is Dana."

I paused. Again, she caught me off guard.

"Hello?" she said when she didn't hear anything.

"Yo. It's Michael. Michael Keith." I figure I could at least tell her who was randomly calling her phone.

"Oh... wow. Hi." She sounded surprised.

"How you doin?"

"I'm doing well. Thanks for asking. I– I honestly didn't think you were going to call." She followed with an uncomfortable laugh.

"My bad. I got a little wrapped up with work and didn't really have the time until now." I didn't wanna tell her I was trying to figure out a better approach than my normal 'let me beat' tactics.

"Oh, ok. I understand. Well, I'm glad you called."

"Yea, I was wondering if you would be

interested in meeting me for drinks at Cortez downtown. I hear they have great live jazz music. Could be a cool vibe for us to get to know each other." I basically regurgitated exactly what Taylor told me a few minutes ago.

"Wow. Yes, of course. I'm interested. When?" She caught me off guard with that one. I quickly moved back to my desk to check my instant messages where Taylor had already dropped the reservation.

"How about tonight at 8:30?" I read directly from the screen.

"Ok, sounds good."

"Oh, and I can come pick you up around 7:45... if you're ok with that." Another line I read directly from the brain of Taylor.

"Yes. That works for me."

"Alright cool. Well um... text me your address and I'll see you later."

I'm not even about to stunt, I had never asked a girl to let me pick her up for a date that I wasn't planning to get no pussy from. That shit was so foreign to me. I usually just have them meet me out and they could ride back with me if they were bout that action. I signed up to escort someone on a date who probably wasn't going to have my dick in their mouth by the end of the night at that shit is just wild to me.

•••

I was fitted in an all-black tailor-made Gucci suit

with a matching Gucci belt with gold buckle, freshly waxed loafers, and gold Rolex. Something fresh but not too much for the new reformed me. I had my barber touch me up just to make sure I was fresh and I had on my fan's favorite cologne. I was looking good, smelling great but feeling better.

I arrived at the address that Dana sent me one minute past 7:45. She didn't even make me come to the door she came right out. I got out and made sure to open the door for her to get in my Benz. Before she got in, she greeted me with a smile and subtly said, "You look nice."

She did too. She had on a long dark green body glove gown and that ass was poking. She had them titties spilling over the top and her hair was out in a curly look with a side-part. Different from the braids she had when I first met her. She smelled great too. Sexy as fuck. I tried to remind myself that I was here to learn about her but I was tryna see what them guts was talking about too.

I closed the door behind her and hopped in the driver's seat.

"This is a nice car." She was looking around at the red leather interior. "I definitely like this style."

"That's right. You're an interior decorator, you into style and stuff."

"Yes, I absolutely am. Design, decorum, and fashion are my passions."

"I can see you got that fashion on lock." I ran my hand across her thigh calling attention to her dress.

She smiled. "Well, thank you. Yea, to be honest,

I didn't know what to wear out with you because when I saw you you were casually dressed. Jeans and button-down but, I got the vibe from you that you could probably dress. Then, I looked up the place we're going to and saw that it was upscale so I figured I should pull off a look. And I'm glad I did, Mr. Gucci suit." She laughed.

I smiled. "You probably would have looked amazing regardless." I was charming, something that comes natural to me.

I could tell she was flattered.

Took us about thirty minutes to pull up to Cortez. I pulled into the valet, allowed my date to hold my arm after she exited from the car, and then we walked in.

"Reservation for Michael Keith," I told the hostess.

"Yes, Mr. Keith, a pleasure to have you dining with us this evening. Your assistant has given us your preferences and your orders have already been placed."

Taylor at it again. *I really need to give that woman a raise.* "Sounds good," I confirmed as they seated us at a quaint corner couch and table set up. Perfect for socializing.

"Your assistant?" Dana asked.

"Yea. My assistant," I repeated back to her. I wasn't sure what she was getting at.

"It's their pleasure to have you dining with them? What are you a professional athlete or something?" She seemed to have just a little concern in her voice so I cleared it up.

"No, baby. I'm not an athlete. And, I'm not sure why they are happy to have me here. I'm assuming because my assistant already ran them a credit card payment." She laughed. I successfully disarmed her.

"So what do you do?"

I knew this would be the first thing we covered. "I'm the Chief Executive Officer of Shut It Down Studios."

"You're the CEO of Shut it Down?!" She repeated back to me in disbelief.

I nodded. I couldn't tell if she was on some groupie shit or not so I let it play out.

"I remember when that small business started years ago and I also remember driving past it earlier this year and saying to myself 'there's nothing small about that place now'. Congratulations on all your success. Such a come up for a young Black man. I hope to do the same with my design business."

"Thank you. Yea our growth has been pretty impressive over the last few years. We just opened the Atlanta location not too long ago."

"Wow. And to think I almost chewed you up for bumping into me on the sidewalk."

I laughed. "Yea you definitely was not giving a brother a break. I hope I'm on your good side now."

"We'll see. So far so good." She had so much personality about her, not to mention she was fine as fuck. Made it easy to sit and talk.

We talked through our three-course meal that

had been hand selected by Taylor and we made it through a whole bottle of wine. We had gotten real close to each other on this small couch. So close that I managed to graze a titty and a thigh. If you ask me, the night was going well.

I drove Dana back to her house and walked her to her front door.

"Michael, it was an absolute pleasure to spend an evening with you." She leaned into me.

"Likewise," I said, looking down on her since she was directly under my face at this point. I took my right arm and wrapped it all the way around her cinched waist, and took my left hand and gently lift her chin. Then, I kissed her so gently I felt her body relax. She laced her lips between mine and when I pulled away she gently bit my low lip, begging me to come back in. I resisted and let her loose from my hold.

"I hope I get to talk to you soon," I said before I walked back to my car.

I got in my whip, watched her get inside safely. Before I drove off, I adjusted my dick in my pants since it clearly switched positions in the last few minutes. Then, I headed home.

14

Couch Chronicles
Mike

"Taylor. Dana wants me to pipe her ass down." This time Taylor and I were out at the mall shopping.

"How do you even know what?" She asked from behind a rack in Nieman's.

"She sent me this sexy ass picture this morning talking about 'Good morning' from her bed and I could tell she was ass naked under them covers."

She laughed. "Ok, she's flirting with you. Sure maybe she would like to have sex with you but the new you respects women even when they being a little slutty."

"The new me wants some pussy. I'm not about to cap. So how we fix that?" I said that so loudly that a shopper near us gasped.

Taylor laughed again. "You think you would still

talk to Dana if you got exactly what you wanted from her sexually?"

I thought about. "If that shit good then hell yea. I'ma run it back a few times."

She shook her head. "And after you run it back are you still interested?"

"Man… I think she dope and I really like our conversations but I can't promise I'ma like her like that if the sexual chemistry not there." I immediately thought about the only woman who had me fiending for her sex because that shit was always interesting, Taya. Then, I came back to reality because Taya was long gone.

"I think you might be ready. And, you're right, sexual chemistry is very important but I just wanted you to learn that there are other features to women outside of sex."

"Sensei, I appreciate all your wisdom," I joked, hugging her from the back as we continued buying the whole mall.

•••

That night, I invited Dana over to chill. She had never been over to my house before now but I was hoping she already knew what I had in mind. My home stayed clean but I made sure to set off the lounge area near my back patio with some candles. And I started the fireplace in the living room just to set the right mood. I ordered Japanese takeout just in case we wanted some food and I pulled out two bottles of warm red cabernet from the wine fridge.

After I showered and took care of my hygiene, I

threw on a leisure set: dark grey soft material sweatpants where I knew my print would be visible and a matching long sleeve shirt fitted enough to show off my arms and my chest. Fresh haircut, smelling good, and oiled up ready for my appointment.

About ten minutes after nine my doorbell rang. I threw on the slow jams on a low volume right before I answered the door.

I opened the front door and Dana was standing in front of me in what had to be the sexiest red tight fitted satin dress that I have ever seen on a woman. She walked past me and right then and there I knew she knew what was up because I could see she didn't have on panties or a bra. *Damn.*

Dana stood in my kitchen sipping a glass of fine red wine, hair pulled back into a puffy ponytail, dark sexy ass skin coated in a layer of body oil, smelling like a fresh bar of soap with both her titties looking at me dead in the face.

"Dana. Look. I can't even lie to you right now. You look good as fuck." I felt the wine kick in.

"I was literally just thinking the same about you."

"I hope this doesn't offend you but I'm trying to get you ass naked on my couch."

She grabbed my hand and led me into the lounge area where I had the candles lit. We placed our glasses on the center table and she forced me to sit by pushing me at my chest. I sat down with legs wide open.

She took one of her spaghetti straps and lowered it past her elbow and then she did the same with the other. I could tell she knew she had the most perfect set of titties just by how she exposed them. My dick grew but I didn't move. I'd seen enough titties in my life to not be pressed. She let the rest of her dress fall off her body fulfilling the first part of my request: get ass naked.

Then, she did the second part and straddled me on the couch. This was pretty much my green light to get as nasty as I please.

She laced her soft as lips between mine gently biting when she felt appropriate. I took both my hands and fully palmed her ass instrumenting the movement that I would need to be able to slide in it effortlessly later.

"You got some big ass titties. You can suck your own nipples?" I was on some freak shit plus I was curious.

She grabbed her right breast and slowly flicked her nipple back and forth with her tongue.

"Damn," I whispered. "Let me taste it." She grabbed both and fed me one at a time. I closed my eyes and enjoyed the soft elements I was pressed against. I moved my hands inward toward her pussy lips all while keeping her ass gripped. I played with her soft wet insides and enjoyed her nipples. She moaned. My first time hearing her moan; before the night was over I was trying to hear her scream.

I took my time with this foreplay because I could tell she was enjoying it. No need to rush it. After I had my slob dripping down from her neck to her titties, I lifted her and laid her across the sofa then I pushed her legs back.

"Hold em right there. You better not fucking move," I ordered her.

"Yes, Daddy." I had her going and she hadn't even experienced the dick yet.

I gently ran my tongue across the full length of her vagina. Bottom to top. I lightly flicked my tongue across the clit, barely grazing it. She sounded off.

Her pussy lips were fat so I could completely close them even though I had her legs spread. I used that shit to my advantage. I was hard and aggressive, sucking and nibbling on the outer lips. Then, I took my tongue and spread them where I would gently kiss and lick on the inner lips. I went back and forth until I saw a clear thick fluid drip through. Dana had yelled my full name many times by the time I made her cum.

"Let them legs go," I demanded. She listened. I wasn't asking her for no permission.

I pulled her down the length of the couch making room for me.

"The only thing you can do with them hands is play with these titties, that's it. Don't try to control my pace or speed, I got this." She nodded and did exactly what I asked.

I slid my pants off and immediately tucked my erect raw dick inside of the wettest thing I have been inside for months. She threw her head back once she realized I was almost all the way inside.

I braced myself on the couch with my left hand and grabbed her thighs with my right hand and I stroked every inch of that pussy. I could tell she wanted to grab me but she followed orders and squeezed her titties instead; which visually only made me want to fuck more. By now, we was both moaning loud as fuck as I fucked a dent into my couch.

I took both her arms and threw them around my neck then I flipped her over on top of me.

"Grab the couch," I told her to brace herself.

I grabbed her thick ass and slid my dick in and out of her forcing her to ride me. Before I knew it, she pinned her hands against my chest and was bouncing nothing but fat ass all over my manhood. I was trapped. My toes balled up as I felt all of her body against me. That shit felt too good.

I broke her hold and pulled her fine ass off me. Then, I bent her across the couch, burying her face in the cushion and then I went back in from the back. Her ass clapped against my abs over and over again. I threw my head back and just moaned cause this pussy was taking my soul away from me. It was a matter of strokes before I pulled out and busted all over her cheeks.

I took her upstairs to my walk-in shower where we rinsed off.

"My body is tingling," she said once we both caught our breath.

"Oh, yea. You liked that?" I pulled her in, holding her body close to me.

"I knew you had some elite dick from the day I

met you. I could see the print through the pants," she laughed.

"So am I Daddy now? Or you were just saying that cause I was making that pussy cream?"

"Oh no, you most definitely are Daddy now. Whenever you want this naked body on a couch you got it."

"Let me get that in this shower then since it's mine now."

"Yes, Daddy."

I tore that ass up one more time as a farewell gift since I was about to be out of town for a little bit. It had been a minute since I clapped some new cheeks in my shower; I forgot how much I fucked with it.

Dana slept curled up in my silk sheets naked, fresh, and clean from the shower that we utilized for its proper usage. I texted Taylor making sure everything was ready for me to fly out in the morning. And, of course with Taylor, everything was already thought through and executed with perfection. I slept good knowing everything was in order.

15

AN OLD BUSINESS PARTNER
Mike

My flight was an early one. I left in just enough time to miss the rain that was coming into the city, early enough that the sun wasn't even awake yet. During my short three-hour flight, I kicked back a few mimosas in my first-class seat, listened to the new album, and caught up on a few emails on my phone. But, mostly, I was just thinking about that couch action I had last night. I kept remembering that bounce back dribbling against my abs on repeat. *Shit... she might be the one.*

My flight landed a little before 9 a.m. with the time difference between zones. I grabbed my bags and then picked up the luxury car Taylor ordered for me. She knows that I hate not being mobile; I need a car no matter where I pull up. Austin was a little different than Miami but one thing they had in common was that thick ass morning traffic. I sat in traffic on Interstate 35 for over an hour just to drive five miles.

"Ok, Michael, you have an event to attend with the owner of the PR company this evening. It's a cocktail type of thing so you need to dress nice and you need to be on time. It starts at 5:30." Taylor spoke to me through the car speaker.

"On time? I don't show up on time," I reiterated.

"This is not one of your little hoochie pool parties where you can come three hours late because that's when the music gets good. The event starts at 5:30 and ends at 8 p.m. It's a weekday. Those people are not there to party, they are there for networking. I advise you to be on time." She was making points.

"Alright, and what's this 'dress nice' comment? I always dress nice."

"Yes but you dress black people happy hour nice during the day time, I need you to wear a Michael Keith at midnight type of fit," she explained. I knew exactly what that meant.

"Alright, that's a bet," I confirmed that I was planning to take her advice.

I showed up to the address that was on my calendar and went up to the top floor. The building was nice. Gold accented fixtures, classy ass high-end furniture; it just smelled like money was being made in this building. When I hit the lobby on the top floor, I was immediately greeted by the hostess.

"Hello. Welcome to Sip and Chat. Are you an

RSVP guest?" This mildly attractive white woman with a bob haircut asked. I knew she liked black men off the bob alone, all white women with bobs prefer black penis.

"Michael Keith," I spoke, checking my cuff links.

"Awesome. You're all checked in, enjoy." She pointed toward the door I was to enter.

The whole place was covered in majorities. They were all over the place, all the men wore the same tired ass grey suitcoat, brown pants combo and all the women had on the professional but not too professional business dresses. Luckily I came to add some sauce to this party with my matte black Giorgio Armani suit, gold links, and blue suede dress shoes.

I grabbed the first champagne filled glass off a tray that walked past me.

There she was. Standing tall, prettier than ever. Tailored business pantsuit, stiletto heels with a beat face. Just fucking perfect.

"Michael! How's it going? So glad you could make it!" Winsdale broke my trance. She was excited to see me. We had only one video conference before this but she had a face that was hard to forget.

"Oh, yea, everything is cool." I couldn't even take my eyes off her and that was clear to Winsdale as she caught my gaze.

"Ah, Miss Roberts. Are you a fan of hers?" She asked, joining my admiration. "She's very popular within this group. A charmer." I was already aware but she continued.

"So much so that she walked into one of my wine downs and wowed me with just her sheer presence. Here let me introduce you." Winsdale grabbed my arm as she charged forward, giving me no time to respond to any of her questions.

"No that won't be necessary –" I tried to stop her.

"Oh, no, I insist. She's a great connection and could be useful to you one day." She had no idea how true that was.

I was trying to gracefully remove the grip of this middle-aged white woman without making a scene but apparently, Winsdale was not skipping arm day. By the time I could get a finger loose, Taya was five feet away from me.

Her mouth dropped as soon as she realized it was me. I did this awkward motion with my hand rubbing my nape and then looked off. I couldn't even stomach making eye contact with her.

'Taya I want to introduce you to one of our newest clients. This is Michael Keith—" Winsdale started but by the time she got to my name Taya was preparing to leave.

"With all due respect, Catherine, I'm uninterested in meeting this person. Please excuse me." She left the conversation taking her champagne glass with her.

She charged through the crowd with a direct path to the elevators. She tapped the button so many times she faded the down arrow printed on it. Right before she got on, she downed her champagne glass then placed it on the tray of a server walking by. I watched her and right before the doors closed, she looked at me. She was furious and I could tell all by just simply looking at her.

"Michael I do apologize," Winsdale jumped in.

"No need. Just an old business partnership with a few rough board meetings. You know how that goes." I tried to clean up the whole situation.

"Well, yes, I surely do," she laughed a little.

"I hope you have plans to mend that relationship. I meant it when I said she is a good connection to have, she's going places," Winsdale bragged.

"Yea, I'm hip."

She was right. I needed to do something about that bridge with Taya I destroyed last winter but tonight, for damn sure, wasn't the night. If looks could kill I would have been buried twice.

16

DON'T CRY OVER SPILLED DRINKS
Taya

I made it to the first floor in record time. When I got out onto the street, I released what felt like fourteen months of pain in one single scream. A scream so loud it echoed.

"Why the fuck is he here?" I paced across the sidewalk right in front of the building.

"He can't be here! Not in my new city with my new network. He just fucking can't be!" I was frantic at this point. I couldn't process what was happening to me quickly enough. Many thoughts were racing through my mind with the most prominent one being the last four minutes of my life. *I probably looked crazy storming out of there. How many contacts saw me with a poor attitude? Why the fuck is he here?!* I knew I needed to go back inside but I didn't want to see Mike's face. I also needed another glass of champagne so I sucked it up and made my way back upstairs convincing myself that I could ignore Michael at least for the next hour.

When I stepped off the elevator on the floor of the event I took a deep breath and went inside. I panned the entire room looking for Mike before I made a single step forward. When I didn't see him, I proceeded with caution. In this particular moment I felt paralyzed by my thoughts. Seeing Mike reminded me of all the anger I was suppressing for him and those thoughts reminded me of all my other previous lessons from men. For most of them, there were always two sides to their coin; there was always bad that came with the good.

•••

For the first eighteen years of my life, I tried to be perfect. Then, I spent the next decade trying to be an unstoppable force. My childhood home is directly in the center on a small cul de sac in this little country ass town in Northern Florida. I grew up with both my parents present, way too present if you ask me. I'm the oldest of two girls. My sister is seven years younger. We own an all-black snickerdoodle, who is more salt and pepper now, named Smoky.

Sounds perfect but it wasn't. My dad was incredibly strict and my mom was notoriously unhappy with her marriage, which led her to cheat. Both of them made it impossible for us to find peace at home. Between physical fights, arguments, and the blatant neglect I found myself outside my home often.

North Florida was basically a breeding ground for humid ass temperatures and sticky days. I would spend most of my summer days with my best friend, Jade, at her house; a home just as nice as mine minus the drama. Her mother was the adult and provider but she worked as an RN overnight so we hosted many functions.

As a fifteen-year-old, I thought it was dope to be hanging out with eighteen-year-olds and young college students. I just thought I was a cool mothafucka.

"There's no way he's going to show up," I expressed to Jade across her kitchen island.

"His homeboy said they were going to slide through later. But I don't know why you're acting like you're even going to talk to him."

"He's talking to Cyn. He not even checking for me."

We were having our daily conversation about Luke McAfee. He was my second real crush after I spent six months dreaming about our school's starting point guard, Tyson Bailey, just to learn that fool was remedial and couldn't solve a math problem if you showed him the answer. I literally gave him the answers to a test once and he still failed.

Luke was a freshman at a community college in my town. I had heard that he was studying biochemistry, which I knew nothing about but he surely was much smarter than my first crush. But naturally, his brain is not what drew me, Luke was fine as fuck. I had mostly seen him from a distance at the mall or basketball games but the day I met him he was actually right in front of me. I use the word "met" sparingly in this context. Really what happened was he was standing in line in front of me at

119

Starbucks. I was looking at his stance from behind and based on his voice I could tell he was at minimum a strong six. Then, he turned around looking smooth over me to wave down his friend to join him in line. He flashed his pretty ass smile showing off the dimple in his left cheek and I just froze. That was the day my investigation skills grew as I worked to learn more about this mysterious man that could have easily not been a mystery had I not forgotten how to use my words.

"You don't even know if that's his girl for real."

Cyn was a senior at our high school. She was considered a bad bitch mostly because she was pretty and social, which made her popular.

"Well, I heard," I responded to Jade.

"I think you need to find out tonight and actually talk to Luke. Since you talk about him all the time," she rolled her eyes.

"If he comes, I'll try," I attempted to present some confidence.

Jade had little faith in me as she averted her attention to her phone.

That night, our kickback grew thick quickly and by 11 p.m., we were at House Party numbers. Although Jade was sixteen and I was fifteen, we never hung with people in our grade.

We both were finishing our sophomore year in high school. We were each other's best friend but occasionally we ran in different circles. She was a basketball player and hung with seniors on the team for obvious reasons. I had two homeboys, who were juniors and athletes, that I preferred to kick it with. Everyone at our newly formed house party was over seventeen and a large majority were in college. With that came drinking, smoking, and tons of sexual experiences.

"Yo, this shit is getting wild!" Jade found me on the

couch with Jermis and Jordan.

"Do you even know all these people?" I asked.

"I was literally about to ask you that."

"I invited Jermis and Jordan that's it," I answered. Jade looked concerned.

"Yea and she damn near forgot to invite me." Jordan was salty because I almost forgot about him.

"Nah, bro if your name not Tyson then Taya not paying you no attention my boy." Jermis thought he was funny. They both laughed. I didn't.

"I'm not even checking for him anymore, so chill." I was spicy.

"Probably because my six-year-old brother can read better than that nigga."

Jordan was a hater. Mostly because he tried to talk to me my freshman year and I told him he wasn't my type then friend-zoned him. I never could figure out why he cared so much; he had plenty of other girls in our school all in his face. He was the starting shooting guard for our basketball team, which meant there were plenty of groupie underclassmen sitting in the bleachers just to see him shoot three-pointers. He was likeable because of his silly demeanor and tall athletic frame but he was just cool to me and it was easier to think of him as a friend.

Jermis was silly too but way more built, he played football and was not at all concerned about me. He had a girlfriend that he was crazy about. She was a cheerleader and they made the perfect jock-cheerleader combo. Between Jordan and Jermis, I knew everything I needed to know about the boys at my school. And being cool with them helped my credibility since I was an unathletic underclassman with good grades.

"Whatever. I know better now." I rolled my eyes.

"Now? What about Keith, Dremond, and Richard? They're off the list too?" Jermis was not about to let this conversation die.

"Bro, Taya is just collecting niggas. I don't think she likes anybody really, she just wanna play with our emotions." Jordan playful nudged me.

"Jermis, why are you even bringing up old shit? All of them you named, I liked last year. Back when I was an immature freshman. I'm a sophomore now. I got taste."

Both of them took me for a joke and started uncontrollably laughing. Right in the middle of this breakdown, I felt a sharp hit in the center of my back as a person fell into me and knocked both of our drinks out of our hands. My mouth hinged open as I watched the liquid seep into my cropped sweater. Just ten seconds ago I was super cute and now I was standing there super soaked.

"Yo, what the fuck?!" I yelled, wiping juice from my forearm.

"Damn. Yo, my bad," this slightly raspy voice spoke.

I looked up and it was Luke. My mouth hit the floor once I realized it was him. I forgot there was juice on my new shirt and all over Jade's floor.

"I'm sorry, shorty." He seemed to be truly apologetic as he grabbed the bottom of my shirt testing to see how much of a mess he actually made. Luke McAfee is touching my crop top! Jordan and Jermis watched me react. Jermis made the "mmm-hmmm there she goes again face" and Jordan just mean mugged because he was forever a hater with me interacting with any other guy.

122

"Come here, let me help," Luke extended his hand for me to grab. Jade nudged me out of my trance and I took his hand and followed him into the hallway to the guest bathroom.

"I'm really trippin right now. I'm usually way cooler than this." I believed him. He closed the door to the bathroom, lifted me to sit on the marble bathroom countertop, and grabbed the decorative towel from the towel rack behind the door.

"No, it's fine. I didn't really like this shirt anyway." That was the first actual sentence I spoke to him. I awkwardly laughed, he smiled.

"It was a good shirt." I could tell he had been drinking but he didn't appear to be drunk.

He wet the towel in the sink and then assisted in making my skin less sticky.

"I'm Taya." I just assumed he forgot to ask with all the chaos.

"Luke." He looked up at me. Little did he know, I was very familiar with him.

He flashed his pretty smile. I had never been this close to him, well at the coffee shop we were this close but his back was facing me. He was much taller than me, even with me sitting on the counter he was still looking down at my small teenaged body. He was holding my arm trying to clear up his mess as I examined his fresh fade, waves, and clean line. He was so fine to me.

I think he could tell I was feeling him because he leaned in and kissed my lips. He just knew he was going to be able to make that move with no problem. I was taken off guard and wasn't sure if I was comfortable with it but it all was happening so fast I couldn't make a decision. I could tell he was experienced,

123

he knew how to kiss, tongue and all. My young ass had barely been kissing boys but I definitely wasn't on full-blown tongue mode. It was all happening way too fast for me. We hadn't even had a proper conversation yet. He didn't even ask for my name and he had his whole tongue down my throat.

He clearly liked my soft full lips because he stopped for a second and ran his fingers over them then he went back in. His aggression picked up and he took off my shirt. His hands roamed my entire body and his lips moved between my mouth and my neck. I couldn't tell if he was uncontrollably into me or if his hormones were taking over his body.

"Luke… I definitely like you but—" I tried to speak but he didn't let me. He shoved his tongue down my mouth forcing me to be quiet. I was sure I was uncomfortable now.

He reached over and turned the light off, pulled my skirt up, and felt my virgin vagina with his fingers. He moaned as he invaded my space. I tried to push his arms back but he was much stronger than my five foot even, one-hundred and twenty-pound fifteen-year-old body could withstand.

The music outside was loud and full of bass. I tried to make noises but between him holding my neck with one hand, his tongue in my mouth, and the loud music I knew nobody could hear me. He unbuttoned his pants with his free hand while using his other hand to keep me in place. Next thing I knew, he was forcing himself inside me. Up until then, I was fighting back trying to get him off me but by this time the pain and pressure were taking over and I just stopped fighting and waited. I was expressionless while he enjoyed himself for what was probably two minutes but felt like an eternity. When he finished, he pulled out and came in his hands. He turned the light back on, washed his hands, and buttoned his jeans.

"I'll see you around, shorty," he said, leaving the bathroom looking at me dead in my face, closing the door behind him.

Time appeared to be standing still as I realized that was my first time. That those four sentences I shared with Luke would be in my memory forever. That those two minutes will always haunt me. I shed a silent cry that later would become the quietest moment of my life. I never told Jade, my parents, or anyone ever. My deepest darkest secret started with a spilled drink and lived in the drain of a bathroom sink.

17

NEVER HAVE I EVER
Taya

"Asya he just was there in the flesh. I was caught off guard. I could barely respond."

"But you're over that asshole and have moved way beyond that trauma." Asya cut up vegetables in our kitchen as we worked toward our teriyaki stir fry.

"Yea, except for when I saw him I was enraged and all my bad memories flooded my brain." I remembered Luke, a story that I kept buried for half my life. "I can't even focus anymore," I admitted, stirring the sauce.

"What about him takes you off your game? You act like he's the first nigga that played you." Her question was valid.

"Asya played is an understatement. He murdered my emotions and ruined my best friend relationship."

"Camille was shady anyway. I told you that in college."

"Yea but still. I wasted so much time with that man and gave him a lot of my attention and love…" I whispered the last part.

"Ohhh you loved him?"

"I mean … something like that."

"And then he fucked you, called you a hoe, fucked your best friend, and embarrassed you in public. Did I leave anything out?"

"Wow. Thanks for the summary," I replied sarcastically as I drained rice noodles. Her comment was real but it hurt all at the same time.

"Just trying to get clarity on why this fool is a topic during our wine and stir fry session. Like, he's not worth the air it takes to complete these sentences. In my mind, he doesn't exist."

"Yea. That was me too. Until Winsdale signed him as a client and asked me to be a mentor to him."

"Ohhhhh well… In that case… you're fucked." She sipped her wine, glaring at me over the top of her glass.

I shot her a sharp look as the doorbell rang. It was our guests joining us for our wine and stir fry session.

"You lucky I gotta answer the door." I glared at her, pointing with the spatula as I went to open the door.

"Who is it?!" I screamed at the closed door.

"Taya you know damn well it's us!" Todd, who

128

had grown to know me all too well at this point, yelled through the door. He had been to our house damn near every weekend since he and Asya started fucking. He brought Brandon with him this time since I always complained about being the third wheel at our dinners.

"How I ain't know you was the police?" I asked a rhetorical question as I opened the door greeting them. Todd playfully pushed my head to the side as he squeezed past me to greet the person he was ultimately here to see. And Brandon stood there with his arms open like he was expecting me to gracefully fall into his very well built upper body. I rolled my eyes.

"You can come in," I curved him.

He laughed. He was used to me being like this with him. I actually think he would have been surprised if I fell into his hands for a warm embrace.

"Glad to see you gentlemen could make it," Asya greeted.

"And you didn't come empty handed. Great signs of home training," I played. Everybody laughed.

"I wouldn't dare walk into your home empty handed knowing the kind of expectations you have, Miss Roberts," Brandon extended a well-received ass kissing compliment. He knew what he was doing.

"Well good. Our Thai stir fry is almost done and the rice noodles are cooling. Can I offer you both a glass of wine?" Asya started pouring.

"You already know. After the day I had at the hospital, I'ma need a whole bottle to myself." I sometimes forget Todd is a doctor.

"What happened?" I was curious.

"Bus crash on 35 today. Crashed into two motorcycles and a convertible. One of the dudes on the bikes came in with damn near his whole arm detached from his body. On the one day I have to do ER rotations, I got the worst accident we've seen all year."

"Damn that's rough, bae. Is he ok?" Asya took a seat at the island next to Todd.

"Last time I checked his arm was stitched back in place but that recovery gone be a bitch." He shook his head.

"Damn and meanwhile I thought I was having a bad day because I couldn't get my code to render," Asya added. We appreciated her attempt to bring back the lighthearted feel of the evening.

"And, Brandon, how was your day? In court or in the office?" I engaged him.

"Court all week this week. Closing in on a fifty million dollar lawsuit. Can't really say much other than that at the moment but this case got a brother stressed," he answered, taking a gulp from his wine glass.

"Sounds like we're all having a rough week so far but the good news is Wine and Stir Fry can commence!" I added all the flavor I had to the conversation as I emptied the wok into our serving bowl. "Everybody grab a plate, your glass, and place at the dining table. Let's get it poppin."

•••

We all sat around our six-seat dining table with the correct portion of stir fry to meet our appetites and a glass full of red cabernet sauvignon, having the most intellectually stimulating conversation a group of highly successful twentysomethings could have.

"He's done nothing for the social climate nor has he lifted a single finger for the Black community. I can comfortably say he does not have an invite to the family picnic. I don't care how many hashtags Black lives matter tweets he gets off." Asya stood her ground on a social media justice worker.

"And just to further that position, not only has he done nothing for our community, he gets his entire following off of the suffering of Black men that fall victim to the justice system. I don't know about y'all but in my hood that is not noteworthy," I added.

"But can we agree spreading awareness is important?" Todd chimed in.

"Important to a degree. We, as a community, have to draw the line between spreading awareness and flat out pandering," Brandon added his two cents.

I snapped my fingers in admiration of his addition. "Please continue, cause that is a word."

"I'm just saying spreading awareness for social issues that we have been aware of since the beginning of this nation like police brutality and flat out racism is neither useful or progressive. I would invite this half-brother to the cookout if he got up and did something for the people. But the man tweets professionally, that's not honorable. As a Black man that fights for a fair judicial system every day in a room full of white supremacists, I can honestly say he ain't putting in no work." Brandon dropped the mic.

"Well… And on that note, I think we can conclude that Brandon is the most woke out of all of us," Asya noted sarcastically. We all laughed.

"Ladies that was a fantastic meal. Thank you for having us." Todd stood up and began gathering the plates. Brandon followed suit.

"Absolutely our pleasure," Asya commented.

"And when she says 'our pleasure', she means we were going to do this anyway so no big deal." Again, we all laughed.

"So now what? A drinking game?" Asya was in the mood for some more entertainment.

"Bruh, I'm too old for flip cup or beer pong. We can just drink if you tryna get drunk," Todd joked.

"No, that's lame. Let's play Never Have I Ever?"

"Wait how does that work again?" I asked.

"You hold up five fingers, one of us asks a question starting with 'never have I ever' and if it's something you've done before, you gotta drop a finger and take a sip," Asya explained.

"So the point is to say things that you haven't done but others probably have so that you can win," Todd added.

"Hmmm ok." I was a little hesitant because there was barely anything I hadn't done but I actually didn't care in this setting.

We all took a seat in the living room on the couch. I brought over the bottle of wine and placed it on the table in the center.

"Ok, who's going first? Brandon." Asya put him on the spot.

He laughed. "Alright. Never have I ever… dated someone outside my race." He looked around the room.

"Define dated…" I needed clarity.

"Dated as in been romantically interested in being in a relationship with a person whilst going on several dates attempting to learn about them," he clarified.

"Oh, cool." I left all five of my fingers up,

"Ok, I'll go next," Asya spoke up. "Never have I ever fucked a person outside of my race." Asya glared directly at me.

I rolled my eyes, picking up my glass. But to my relief, so did everyone else. We laughed.

"Look I fucked this Mexican dude once when I was in Miami. He was a papi though. A fine young thang," I admitted.

"Todd you go."

"Alright. Never have I ever smashed the parent of someone I was romantically involved with." He looked around. So did everyone else. And, then, I took the leap of shame and lowered my finger before grabbing for my glass.

"Taya!" Asya gasped.

"Look. His father was eyeing me the whole time. And again the man was fine. His son wasn't cutting it anymore." I felt bad but it was the truth. Everyone was rolling at my stories. I was embarrassed.

"Ok, my turn, hell." I jumped in.

"Be careful now, it's supposed to be something you haven't done before." Brandon was trying to be funny.

"Ok... how about never have I ever been a part of an orgy." I looked around.

Everybody but Asya stayed still. Finally, I wasn't the freak in the room.

"It was once, in college. An accident really," she explained.

"Was it an orgy or a train?" I could tell Todd was concerned.

"It was – an all-girl orgy. Four of us."

"Oh, shit! Ok, now we talking!" Brandon took a sip just off the thought.

It was clear that the vibes in the room were shifting. We had one too many glasses of wine at this point and the mischievous sex adventures of Taya was making everybody think.

Asya and Todd wrapped themselves up betwixt each other and before I could blink, Asya was being stripped of her clothes with intense passion.

It was at that moment that I remembered how good Brandon slanged dick. I looked over at him to see that he was already staring at me.

"Let's go to my room," I said and I grabbed his hand, leaving Asya and Todd behind. I took him to my large bedroom with a bay window overlooking the lake. By the time we got up to my room, I was expecting him to be all over me but instead, he sat on the edge of my bed.

"You not feeling me like I'm feeling you?" He finally put two and two together.

It took me about four solid seconds of thought to decide if I was going to be brutally honest or keep him in the dark.

"I do think we have differences in the intensity of our feelings." I sat down in the large chair in the corner of my room.

"Difference as in you not feeling me at all. Huh?" He needed more detail from me.

"Honestly... I was. But you started applying pressure and that's just turning me off. But I can admit that your sex game is elite."

"So, not likely that I can make you my woman. But you might let me beat every now and then?"

"Exactly." I smiled.

He laughed. "Well shit. Why you ain't just say that?"

He proceeded to pick me up and slay me in between my sheets. And it was on that night I could say "Never have I ever curved a man and got A1 sex all in the same night."

18
BURNING BRIDGES
Mike

"So, tell me how it's going?" Taylor called to wake me up.

I stretched across my hotel bed before I even tried to respond.

"It's cool. I guess," I said vaguely.

"Uh oh. What's going on, Michael?"

I sat up in bed and repositioned myself.

"I kinda saw Taya."

"What?! Kinda?"

"Well, yea. I saw her at Winsdale's office. Apparently, she's a partner."

"Oh, my god."

"Yea."

"See this is exactly why you can't burn bridges—" Taylor was finding her voice with me more and more every day.

"Taylor. I know… ok… shit is definitely fucking me up." I talked through her rambling.

"You have to reconcile that relationship."

"She's not going to talk to me. I mean hell I wouldn't talk to me."

"So the plan is to avoid her?"

"I can't." I rubbed my head. "Winsdale specifically wants me to work with her."

"You need to talk to her. Period."

I rubbed my head. "So how's everything in the office? Please change this subject."

I got out of the bed and placed my phone on speaker and set it down. I knew that question would prompt her to ramble. I dropped a few "yea" and "ok cool" in the conversation just to keep her going. I got to the point where I don't even need to really listen to her because she makes almost everything work without me. But she likes to get shit off her chest so I make time for Taylor daily.

"…which brings me to this branding topic. Your increased brand perception can elevate the Atlanta office. So, I really need you to make this happen, Michael. Like seriously…" she prompted me to listen.

"I'ma figure something out Taylor. But, I don't have a plan right now, ok?"

"Sound good. Well, I need to go but you know how to find me." We ended that conversation.

I had way too many thoughts going through my mind. I was busy trying to even get started on this Austin task and then the thought of having to unburn a bridge I purposely burned just made me stress even more. After I paced the room a few dozen times I made a phone call to Rashad; I remembered he told me he relocated to Austin. We set up some time to catch up today.

I took my rental from my hotel to a cigar bar in the city. Not that it really mattered but I came fitted for any occasion. Black fitted slacks, fresh crispy black Gucci tee, brown casual but dressy shoes, all gold jewelry: chain, Cuban bracelet, bottom grill.

"Say, bro. I see you, my boy," a compliment coming from Rashad.

"Nah, bruh I'm tryna get like you. You got em all," I returned the favor.

We took a seat at the bar, picked our cigars, and ordered our drinks of choice. The perfect middle of the day, in the middle of the week activity.

"What's been going on, young one?" Rashad and I haven't talked since he was interning in Miami.

"Shit. Spent a few months out in New York last winter built a few key partnerships and then got an offer out here. Thought it was a solid move so I took it."

I was remembering when he was having a hard time starting his career and how he's taking off.

"My man, you know it's always a space for you at Shut It Down. Just say the word."

"I might have to take you up on that one day."

Then, I watched him get visibly uncomfortable he took a sip of his straight cognac and I mimicked him out of habit.

"Alright. You know we have been cool for a minute now and I appreciate every single opportunity you created for me…" he started.

"Bro, what's up? You talking like you fucked my bitch or something" I laughed and he finished his whole drink. I stopped laughing.

I changed my demeanor to indicate that I was waiting for him to finish.

"Don't react immediately, let me explain."

"Bruh… say that shit." I was getting frustrated with his hesitation.

"When I was in New York, I ran into Taya," he started. My face immediately showed disdain.

"And you probably fucked cause she easy as fuck."

"I'm not tryna talk down on her."

"Oh, so you did crack that," I laughed.

"I cuffed."

My whole face changed into confusion. "What? You do know that's my ex?"

"Is she? Cause how the story was told to me you dropped her and you were never official." I didn't say shit.

"I'm not trying to dismiss that y'all have history. This is why I'm bringing it up. But I know y'all couldn't make it work and I did curve her when I first met her in Miami. But when I saw her in New York I just knew that was destiny."

I know this fool not talking to me about destiny at this cigar bar.

140

I finished my drink. "Well, she's old news to me at this point so good luck with y'all relationship." I was salty.

"We broke up," he said while flagging down the bartender.

"Then why you even bringing it up?"

"Because I respect you, Mike."

I took a second to think about the conversation and then I remembered Taylor lecturing me about burning bridges. With all the details on the table, I had to admit I did fumble my bag with shorty and it wasn't like he was with my girl when she was mine and he did approach me like a grown ass man.

I took a deep breath. "I appreciate you, fam." I extended my hand. We shook on it and went back to drinking.

I spent the next few hours getting Rashad drunk and listening to everything that happened with him and Taya. What I did to her I didn't really think his one cheat was comparable to what I did to her at all. I also wouldn't have told on myself; she would have had to catch me in the act if she wanted to find out. Ironically enough that has happened to me before. Rashad seemed remorseful but was convincing himself that he didn't deserve her after what he had done. And I for sure wasn't about to be the person that would convince him otherwise. After we drank nearly half a bottle of cognac on our own, I felt like I had enough info about Taya's whereabouts to figure out how I was going to approach rebuilding this bridge.

19

TWO MINUTES
Mike

"You have a very important dinner on your calendar tomorrow night. Make sure you grab your suit out of the cleaners. I'd totally do it for you, but you're in Texas still. And I'm not—" Taylor kept reminding me how much I depended on her on a day to day basis as I continued my mission in Austin.

"Yea. I got it. Don't worry about that. What I got on my plate today?" I asked her to shift the subject matter. I was in my hotel room bathroom, ass naked with a towel wrapped at the waist as I brushed my teeth.

"You just have a few meetings in the office. Nothing major. Your entire afternoon is free. You should take advantage of this and knock out some of the tasks you've been putting off."

I didn't immediately respond, I thought about it

for a second. Taylor, knowing what kind of person I am, gave me a moment of silence to process.

"Can you do me a favor?"

"Of course. My literal job description is to fulfill all your requests."

"Book a reservation for two at the most impressive restaurant you can find in this city for 11 p.m.."

"On it. May I ask who the second seat is for?"

"I'll tell you tomorrow if I can pull off what I'm thinking. I'll say less for now."

She laughed a little. "Sounds good to me. Let me know if you need anything in the meantime."

"Nah just keep holding everything down on the home front. Use my credit card to buy yourself something nice. That's a formal request and I expect it to be done." I was serious.

"I hear you loud and clear."

I had my driver drop me off at Steamers, a lil hip-hop joint downtown. To describe it, the club was two stories, a fair size, and newly renovated, which made people feel like they needed to look nice to get in. The line was wrapped around the side of the building but, you know me, I walked right in that bitch. I spotted the bouncer a fifty piece for his troubles and not another question was presented to me as I made my way inside.

There were quite a few bad hoes sprinkled around the club. I guess it is true what they say about Texas, everything is bigger, because all I saw was thick women in tight clothes. Saw this fine yella thang staring me down like I was a peanut butter cookie and she ain't ate all day. And, though she was bad, she wasn't my type; she was wearing a cheap ass outfit, her wig was lifting up in the front. Strong pass from me. I hovered over the bar not trying to make eye contact.

After an hour, I finally saw Taya walking up to the bar looking fine like she always does. A short fitted black dress, red bottoms that complimented her legs, hair out and wavy; just fine. She took a seat. I immediately grabbed the bartender.

"You see that woman at the end there… wavy, big hair, bring her a glass of the best Prosecco you have to offer. On me."

He nodded and proceeded to intercept his partner who was about to take her order. Then, he dropped off the order as I asked him to. She looked up and around but never in my direction. I just observed her for a second, collecting my thoughts on what I was about to say to her.

The whole club appeared to be moving in slow motion from the moment I decided to approach her. The club was thick; dance flow was covered and in action. The bar was crowded with very little standing room but I managed to get close enough to gently touch her elbow just enough for her to turn around.

She looked shocked and then immediately followed with pissed. But it was hard for her to move away quickly.

"Don't be like that." I don't know what I was

thinking.

"Don't tell me how to be, Michael."

"What I meant to say is that's unfortunate that this is your natural reaction to me."

"Disgust? Is that the reaction you're picking up?" She was being funny now.

"Yea. That's what's coming through."

"Then good. I'm doing this right." She turned around and downed the rest of her drink. I flagged the bartender for another round.

I leaned over her right shoulder. "Can I talk to you?" I spoke directly in her ear.

"No." She didn't even look at me.

"Two minutes. We clearly got some shit we both need to figure out let's just knock this conversation out right quick. Two minutes."

I could tell she was thinking about it because she didn't immediately say no this time. The bartender came back with our drinks.

"Two minutes?" She finally responded.

I nodded. I grabbed her hand to help maneuver her through the crowd, protecting her from all the drunks. I had already reserved a booth in the back of the club that fit four people, but I just needed the space to talk to her.

"So you think you're smooth? Having surprise drinks delivered, conveniently having a quiet section for us to talk in." She was already skeptical.

"You know I'm a smooth nigga, in general." I wasn't about to downplay myself.

She sipped her drink. "Your two minutes has

already started, smooth nigga."

"Yea, so straight to business. I came out here to get my public image together. I'm partnering with Catherine's firm and she thinks you are the best person for the job. She keeps describing you as the best public relations and marketing guru to hit this market in a long time. She won't pair me with anyone else."

"So it looks like you're fucked. I'm not working with you. Plus I'm leaning more into focusing on my tech business, public relations is my old business." She sat with her legs crossed and one arm folded over the other, holding her champagne glass.

"You really gone let me take an L like this? Instead of getting the commission that you deserve for being the best to offer in this city?" I was trying to wear her down.

"Excuse my brashness, but I don't give a single fuck about you or an L. And I don't work for Winsdale, I work with her. I don't follow orders from anybody." She did not crack a smile.

I sat back on the couch, looked off into space trying to figure out if I was willing to let anybody talk to me like they lost their mind or if I was about to say fuck it.

I took a sip of my cocktail. "Let me say this and, then, you can go. I recognize what I did to you was wrong and I'm sincerely apologetic about that. You didn't deserve to be treated like anything other than the graceful woman that you are. One day, you'll see the flaws you also had in our encounters together but I don't need an apology from you. I'm moving on and off this topic. If you want to continue to be mad about it that's unfortunate. The last thing I'ma say is you of all people know I don't let people talk to me in the way you talk to me now. So I'ma excuse myself before I say some shit I regret. You can enjoy this section. I didn't come here to party." I finished my drink, stood up, and left without looking back.

20

PICKING UP THE PIECES
Taya

My mind flashed back to the moment I was sitting across from him at the quaint restaurant back in Miami. I remembered all the shit he dropped on me that day without a care in the world. I thought about how that moment was the beginning of the end of my friendship with Camille. How days after he gave me that backstabbing news I pulled up on Camille at her job and beat her ass for the culture. How I was so enraged at the two of them that I left my job in the middle of the week to take a trip out to New York. How I basically rearranged my whole fucking life based off of this one man. How that one moment was such a defining truth for the type of woman I was about to grow into. In an undesirable way, I learned that I was lacking humility; believing that I was above contempt, above misfortune.

But, most importantly, I learned that the barrier of impenetrable resistance that I, at the moment believed, was to protect me from shitty people only protected me from people who were unable to finesse accordingly. I learned that though I knew a lot, I knew nothing. He broke me down and left me in pieces.

And here he was standing in front of me, needing me. Then, I thought about it for another second, is this karma? Am I getting my chance to shit on my haters? Or was this the continuation of the less that I was already learning? Or was this the opportunity I needed for closure so that I could move on.

Either way, I thought about what Winsdale said and I thought about the commission check.

"Mike. Wait…" It took everything inside of me to swallow the large amount of pride I had been holding on to all year.

He turned around and looked at me.

"I'll take on the project." I agreed to it because I needed it for my own professional reasons. Winsdale would sign over the permit for my location if I did her this one last favor and represent her new client. She claimed she had no PR reps with skills that matched the portfolio of Shut It Down Records and she had already made a deal. She knew I had years of experience in marketing and asked me for the favor. Really what she meant is that she had no Black PR agents to pick up the project and I was quite literally her "one black friend."

"Oh shit. All I had to do was put my foot down huh?" He was cocky. I was irritated by his words and my face was showing it.

"No. All you had to do was finally be a decent person." I shut him up.

He stood there making the face he makes when he is unmoved by anything you are saying. I could just tell that he was pleased with the fact that I accepted his offer.

"And before you get any ideas, this is not a peace treaty. I still hate you with a passion. I'd just like to hurry up and send your ass back to Florida," I was sassy as I finished my drink. I meant that too. I felt like hate was a strong emotion but for the kind of love that I imparted and bestowed upon him and Camille, my love had naturally evolved into hate.

He threw his hands up. "I figured that much."

I turned around and left his section because I didn't need his champagne or section bribes to try to get back into my good graces. After thinking about it... I scurried back and grabbed the champagne bottle because why the fuck not. I could feel him watching me walk away and I made it my job not to pay him any additional attention. I had already given him far too much.

21

SAYING LESS
Mike

That was easier than I thought it would be. I was expecting a drink to be thrown or at minimum to be called somebody's trifling ass nigga. Outside of the sass and the heavy hesitation that was a smooth deal, if you ask me.

On my way out the front door, this little slim joint grabbed me asking for my name. Her titties were sitting up on her chest but she was definitely all the way in the slim category. Slim and cute, though. With curves in all the right places. I wasn't mad at it. Warm brown skin fitted in a snug tight faux leather dress. I could easily tell she came out tonight intending to bag some quality dick. She shot her shot at me, flashing her likable smile; little did she know she didn't really have to do much to get me on this night.

"Let's go to dinner." I thought about the dinner reservations I made thinking my plans with Taya would end on a better note. Slim shorty with the titties and little booty was cute enough. Plus she wasn't shy, which gives me the impression she would be fun to kick it with.

She accepted my offer, allowed me to escort her out of the club, and let me drive her to the restaurant. She was chatty as fuck the whole way to the spot. Only thing I paid attention to was her name, Jess or Jaz. *One of those.* Everything else that came out of her mouth was unimportant to me. My only purpose for coming out tonight had been accomplished and everything else that happened was a bonus. I was about to eat a good dinner, get a drink, get some pussy, then crash.

"So, Money Mike, you don't say much," she called for my attention. Outside of telling her my name in the car and answering her trivial questions so she could figure out my zodiac sign or whatever she was on, I hadn't said much of shit.

"I'm quiet. I don't talk much," I lied. Truth was, she lucky she was cute because I should have left her in the club. I honestly was thinking about my last moment with Taya on repeat. I grabbed her hands as a compromise to show her I was being entertained then I leaned in. "Let's go kick it at my spot." I motioned my head to signal that I was ready to go. She wanted to do whatever I wanted to do.

She had a deep throat and liked using her hands. I like my head all neck with no hands but I'm not picky either. She took off her top and bra, exposing herself. I sat back in my seat, relaxing with my head back as she covered my dick with her spit.

After I got my nut and she swallowed it all, I made up an excuse about not wanting to have sex with her too soon. I got her number, a number I wasn't planning on using ever, and, then, called her an Uber. She picked up her clothes and covered up her body. I was pulling up my shorts.

"I had a good time with you, Mike. Call me," she said on the way out the door. I hit her with a head nod, standing at the door with just some hoop shorts on.

22

NEXT ORDER OF BUSINESS
Taya

Our hand-picked finely finished furniture was being unloaded off the moving truck into our new office location. Four stories, ten thousand square feet, a gallery-style lobby on the first floor, and two large executive offices on the top level. All sitting at the corner of one of the busiest streets in Austin's new tech hub.

My first day in my new office was hectic. The movers were probably the biggest form of traffic. Between them and all the small logistical things we needed to set up: mail couriers, internet, plumbing, our business neighbors popping in to be nosey. And, to add to the level of crazy that was happening around me, my new assistant started today. I remembered how long it took me to break in a new assistant at my last job. I ran two of em out of the building before I had a decent one that could remember my coffee preference and take a good phone message.

Shelly. That was her name. Shelly was a middle-aged black woman, a little heavier than I'd ever like to be, with a short Halle Berry cut that really suited her round face and glasses that I could tell she needed at every second of the day.

"Miss Roberts... uh... you don't mind if I call you Taya, do ya?"

I looked over at her from the other side of my office that had barely two items in it to reply very drably "I suppose."

"Well... Taya... we will need to get to getting on getting to know each other." She paused. "That's a mouthful." Then she laughed uncomfortably. "The more we know about each other the more smoothly this lil relationship here will work."

I again looked so unmoved by her commentary. "I couldn't agree more." I didn't even look up from my iPad.

"So what's your biggest pet peeve?" She intensively took a seat on one of the closed boxes."

"People forcing themselves to learn about me is probably number one." She picked up on my attitude and slowly closed her notebook. Her face looked puzzled as she tried to figure out what was the next most appropriate question to ask me without pissing me off.

I jumped in to help her. "Here's two very

important things you need to know about me. One, I hate with the most intense passion to be double booked. My calendar needs to be appropriately scheduled to allow me to be at every meeting on time without distraction. This means I need a five-minute buffer before and after everything scheduled. The second thing, nobody just walks into my office, including you. People who want to see me need to be on my calendar. I treat my time like the valuable commodity that it is." Shelly was taking more notes than she was prepared to get from her biggest pet peeve question.

"Next order of business" I allowed her to finish her first note before I started again "I'll be in the office by 6:30 a.m. every day and I expect you to be here too. I work twelve hour days so I'll likely leave around 6 p.m., I do not expect you to stay as long. It's up to you when you lunch, break, or whatever but you need to do those things in accordance with what works best for my schedule. Whatever time of day you are planning to clock out is when my meetings need to stop. Is that clear?" I paused.

"So, let me get this straight. Start time is non-negotiable but let's say I wanted to take a thirty minute lunch and head out of here at 3 p.m. every day you would be cool with that?" She followed up.

"If my schedule permits it, I don't see a problem."

"Oh cool. That works for me. I'm trying to get

into Zumba and there's this 3:30 class I've been trying to get into but my old boss was not as flexible as you are, Miss Taya. I like you already." She was happy. I smiled.

The rest of my day was fast-paced. I didn't get a chance to catch my breath until Shelly called over our two way intercom that was installed right after my desk was delivered this afternoon.

"Hey, Miss Taya."

"Yes," I responded. I was knee-deep in some legal documentation I needed to send back over to Brandon.

"You have a visitor in the lobby. He says he's a client but we haven't gotten that far in the onboarding process. You got clients, girl?" She was dead ass serious. I laughed.

"I'm coming." I kept it short and walked outside of my office. Shelly's desk was on the fourth floor in-between mine and Aysa's. The fourth floor set up was purely lounge-style outside of our two offices. Two large plush purple couches, fine colorful artwork was being hung in that very moment, vibrant grey for the rugs, and a few coffee chat-style glass tables set up in each corner. Once we finished having the surround sound installed we would play soft natural tones throughout to give off a chill atmosphere and vibe.

I walked up to Shelly's desk. "Here's your next lesson, downstairs that's Michael Keith." I could see him through the surveillance monitor.

"Girl, that man is fine. I went down there to

make sure it wasn't just someone tryna play games. I wasn't about to call you with no nonsense, but let me tell you, whoever he is, if nonsense is what he served, I would like to purchase two" she snickered.

I smiled. "Well. I suppose he is fine—"

"And well dressed and polite and the man smells good as I don't know what. Whew. Is that yo client or yo man? Cause I ain't mad at ya, sis." She cut me off.

"He's a client, trust me. So like I was saying, that's Michael Keith. I'm working with him on a little PR project. But, what I wanted to say is: make sure he gets a formal appointment with me; no more than once a week and none of these random pop ups." I tried to get back on task.

"Mmm-hmm. I hear you. I wouldn't want that fine man up in here every day. I'd need to go home every lunch just to take a cold shower."

I walked past her to the elevator and took it to the lobby floor. Our lobby was an open space and eventually would have seating and helpful content for our new clients but for now, it was just an empty greeting desk because I hadn't hired a host yet.

"There she goes." Mike greeted me.

"We had an agreement you'd only be around when we had a formal appointment," I stated, folding my arms.

"Yea except we never actually scheduled anything. And seeing that I don't have a new phone number for you and the only way I can even get close to getting contact with you is Winsdale who might I add, graciously gave me the address to your new office location, here I am." He made points.

"I understand. Well, I am busy right now."

"I can see that. All I want is to get something on the calendar and I'll let you go." He raised his hands as a symbol of peace.

"How about Wednesdays? Weekly at 11 a.m. until I've completely convinced the world you are a stand-up gentleman. Which shouldn't be hard because I am the best at what I do. So, four weeks tops; that includes analysis turn around." I pulled out my phone to check the calendar as I humbly bragged.

He couldn't help but laugh. "I knew I was in the right hands. Wednesday or any day for that matter works for me. I'm only here for this and I'm trying to get back to Florida and get back on my regular schedule. You feel me?"

He legitimately seemed like he was about his business with me, no bullshit.

"Sounds like we have a plan. I'll see you in a few days. Have Taylor email me all of your digital footprints, this includes social accounts, websites, media coverage, etc." I grabbed his phone from his hand and updated my contact information. "I added my professional email and work number. See that she gets that info to me before Wednesday." I handed him his phone back.

"Yea, boss. I got you." He saluted me and then left out of the tinted glass doors that led right to the streets of downtown.

162

Shelly was right; he did smell good.

23

THREE MILLION
Mike

"You stalked her at a club, hid in the shadows like a creep, secretly bought her a drink, and then approached her when you knew she didn't have an escape route?" Taylor echoed back to me over the phone that night with Taya.

"Well when you say it like that you make it sound weird."

"The only reason it's not weird is because you are attractive. Let you be somebody's crusty looking uncle and you might have gotten pepper sprayed." She wasn't wrong. I did get away with a lot of shit just because I know I'm attractive.

"Man regardless I did what I had to do. Now I just need to finish this project. Oh, that reminds me can you shoot over my digital shit to Taya before our 11 a.m. meeting?"

"That was done yesterday. Her assistant reached out to me asking I send material twenty-four hours in advance. I knew Taya was about her business but that's really an understatement. That woman does not miss a beat when it comes to getting things done. Oh, and her new assistant is super cool."

I thought about all the times I would get her voicemail because she refused to take personal calls when she was at work and now I'm on the other side of it as a professional contact. One of the main reasons I ever even liked that woman the way I did was because of how she handled her business. But this time, I was focused on getting my shit together. I sunk that ship a long ass time ago anyway. I was aware.

"Say, Taylor, this Dana on the other line. I'll talk to you later and let you know how everything goes." Then, I switched over to FaceTime.

"There she goes," I answered the call.

Dana was on the other side looking like a freshly mixed smoothie in a silk black robe with her hair pulled back.

"I see I have to call you to ever get a word in with you." She seemed a little annoyed but not enough to call me regularly and allow me to miss out on looking at her fine ass.

"You know it's not even like that. I finally got that person I was telling you about to work with me. It

166

just was a lot of upfront investment. Please accept my apology."

"I'll allow it. I think I'm a little cranky because I haven't had a couch session with you in a minute. Or a shower session." She smiled.

"You already know when I'm back that's my first order of business. You, a whole bottle of body oil, and my sheets."

"You gone need a whole new sheet set fucking with me."

"Shit, fuck them sheets." She started laughing.

"I miss you. Come back to Miami."

"A few more weeks and I'ma be back in that thang like I never left."

•••

Vuu: Software and Media Firm, was printed on the sign on the front of Taya's office. A sign that wasn't there a few days ago. *I see she's working.*

When I stepped inside the first floor was completely furnished with complementary nude and earth pallets. There were more couches another obvious change from the last time I was here and there was a receptionist to greet me.

"I have a meeting with Taya."

"Just a moment... Hey, Shelly, Taya has an appointment on the first floor... Yes, he does smell good... Mmm-hmm that too... Ok, I'll send him up." She smiled, hanging up the phone. "You can go up to the fourth floor, elevator is down the hall to your left."

"Thanks." I didn't know what all that was about but I followed the directions.

"Mr. Keith. I can call you Michael?" I remembered Shelly from the first time I came. As soon as I stepped off the elevator she grilled me like she was the IRS.

"Mike works too." I was direct as I straightened the buckle on my belt.

"Well, ok, now, Mike. You don't wanna get too informal with me now." She laughed with her tongue out.

I followed her to an office in the corner. The fourth floor of this building was serene, calm, cool, and very nicely decorated. Shelly opened the door for me and I walked into Taya's big ass corner office. She was on the phone and signaled to me that she needed just one more minute to wrap it up.

"Absolutely. Of course, I understand the hesitation. Let's do this. I'll have my assistant send you our media kit and you can take a look at our offering at your leisure. Give me a call back when you're ready. Sound good? Ok. It was a pleasure. Thanks."

"Shelly, send them the media kit and then schedule a follow-up email for four days." Shelly took the note as Taya spoke and then left. Taya motioned me to join her at her desk.

She browsed through her laptop, took a second to look up at me, then browsed for a few more seconds.

"I'm surprised you even get new customers and clients. Your online presence is trash. Excuse my

168

bluntness."

"I never really needed that online shit. My name ring bells." I wasn't offended.

"Yea but that approach will keep you at the current level you're at. From Taylor's email, the goal is to get new clients in Atlanta. A city you're not from nor do you live in. You're going to need a marketing campaign," she replied.

"You the boss. Tell me what I need to do." I leaned back in the plush seat.

"I'm working on that now. What's your budget like?"

"You know I got the bread."

She looked up at me. "That's not what I asked you."

"I need a booked studio on opening day for the entire week. That's something like three hundred sessions."

"Three hundred?" her eyebrows raised. She took notes.

"Yea I got a big ass stu. About fifty private studio rooms, fully equipped."

"That's a lot of clientele, Mike. Especially on opening day. S.I.D. Miami is doing about two hundred a week. I'm looking at the numbers now." She tried to get me to catch her drift. I understood.

"Yea. I know. That's exactly why I was in the club buying you bottles and shit to get you to help me." I threw my hands up. She covered her mouth, laughing at my realness.

"There's good and bad news. Good news: Atlanta has a huge market for this type of service. Bad news: all the major labels are in Atlanta, even more so than they are in Miami."

I folded my hands and looked up at the ceiling.

"Alright. I'll set the budget at a million. I'm betting big on this spot."

"Add a couple more million and we can host a festival." She turned around her iPad. "Look. Here's the pitch to host a Hip-Hop festival right in the city. Pay a line-up of headliners and feature the natives. For the badges of entry, we offer an exclusive pass that also includes a fee for studio time at S.I.D. Atlanta. There'd also be general admission and an in-between experience. We release a series of videos with coverage of you as you plan the festival; showing your personality, talent, and style. We host the event; promoting S.I.D. on literally everything. Tents, stages, t-shirts, posters, all branded for the business." She took a breath. "And so far, at this scale, I'm projecting it to cost a little over four million. But I could probably pull all my strings and get to three. What do you think?"

"Damn this could work. What kinda profit we talking?" I wanted to know about the money.

"That depends on the venue we book but we're easily doubling the cost. You'd, of course, need to pay me as well."

I had to lighten the mood a little bit and laugh. "Well, like I said, you know I got the bread."

"Say less."

We chopped it up for the duration of the meeting. Most of it was her telling me what I needed to do and who I needed to contact but she had all the logistics on lock. I liked her plan.

24

SLOW DANCE
Taya

"Did you say million? You never told me the man was a millionaire," Asya shouted over the blender as she juiced.

"I told you he owned Shut It Down Records," I followed up after she turned off the juicer.

"Yea but you know how niggas claim they own some shit but really be just like the cousin to the assistant manager or some shit." I laughed so hard.

"I can't believe you think I'd fuck such a scrub. Please put some respect on my last name, baby." I was fake sassy. "Besides, I wasn't even positive he had million millions until today. I thought he had like a million. He just bought a fifty studio facility. That shit is expensive." I was still shocked.

"Remind me again why you not his girl?"

I mugged her so tough. "You literally just three fucking weeks ago was like *'Taya you need to get over that trifling ass nigga'.*" I mimicked her voice

"You didn't say said trifling ass nigga was a real deal millionaire. Bitch the amount of trifling you deal with from a man correlates to the number of dollars in his bank account. I know you took trigonometry."

"Bitch that is not no damn trig." I shook my head and then I moved across the kitchen to grab the wine and poured myself another glass.

"Whatever. I try to teach yo ass something and look how you treat me." She mimicked my pettiness.

A knock at the door cut our conversation short.

"Oh shit. That's Callum. I'm going out with him tonight." I said kind of under my breath and very quickly to Asya followed by me running over to the full body mirror in our hall to check how I look.

"You're going on a date with Callum? What about Brandon?" She switched topics so quickly.

"I told you I curved him."

"But I thought he was beating the brakes off your Benz," she whispered loudly.

Callum knocked again. "He did. He is. But I curved him. Look, it's complicated. I'll tell you the story later. I'm leaving. This is awkward."

I lightly jogged over to the door, greeted Callum, and slid out the front door before Asya asked any more questions.

•••

We sat in the corner of a restaurant at a table set

for two overlooking the city. I felt a little embarrassed because I didn't dress to impress. I was still wearing a pair of fitted black jeans, a black boyfriend t-shirt, and a pair of brown heeled ankle boots. Luckily, I look great in everything but, still.

"I'm actually surprised you agreed to this." Callum always spoke so calmly, very balanced. He was always so poised. Even the day he asked me to go out with him. We were doing a jog around the lake and after we had stopped and started stretching he just said it. *I'd love to talk to you over dinner. Just the two of us.* He looked at me directly in my face, no hesitation.

"Why be surprised?" I sat across from him very interested in his answer.

"I didn't know what to expect or how you would respond to me trying to get to know more about you. You never gave me hints you were interested,"

"You never gave me hints you were interested either." I was partly serious, partly flirtatious.

"I didn't. It took me a minute to realize how great you are. I apologize for the delay." He smiled.

Callum had so much going on for him as far as looks are concerned. Very grown man demeanor. Light sprinkle of salt in his clean-cut beard. Great teeth. Contagious smile with subtle dimples right at the corners of his mouth. Long eyelashes. Almond eyes. But he also had nerd vibes. Tall and lanky. Large hands that he didn't always know what to do with. Simple and basic dress because he probably couldn't point out high fashion in a high fashion magazine. All these things together, he was a pleasure.

"Apology accepted." I returned the smile. I could tell he loved it when I smiled. It made him smile but his smile made me smile. It was all too much.

"I really want my own garden after seeing yours." Yes, this is where we were in conversation. Knee deep in botany after a few good rounds of "which show is better?".

"You have the space for it. But you don't have any time to take care of a garden, you're a busy woman."

"Ugh tell me about it. I'm always working. And that's why I want a garden. To sit outside at night overlooking the lake." I gazed off.

"You could always use mine. I'm just waiting for the day you remember I'm right next door."

"Are you implying I don't pay you any attention?" I leaned into the table,

"Not imply. I'm directly saying you forget I exist until I remind you." He leaned in as well.

He wasn't wrong. Up until now, Callum was not on my radar.

"Well… like you said I be busy." I shrugged a little.

"True. Except you made time for Rashad, Brandon, and random dude you met at the coffee shop." We both laughed. *Wait until he hears about Mike.*

"That's the last time I tell you anything."

"Please don't let that be the last time. I'm just giving you examples. You giving all the wrong people your time."

"Oh and you're the right one."

"I can neither confirm nor deny but I can say I'm not a bad guy to try out."

His smile made me want to say yes to anything he suggested.

"I don't mind giving you a try."

He reached his hand over the table. I sat up in confusion then I trusted him and took his hand. I followed him to the dance floor near the pianist as he gently placed his left hand firmly around my waist and laced his fingers through my right hand. We caught the vibe and slow danced in the middle of the restaurant like no one else was there. He was so smooth on the dance floor and easy to follow. Being with Callum felt like being lost on an island with one cool ass person. His calm presence was relaxing. We danced for a few songs then sat by the fireplace finishing our wine. By now, I was on glass number five after pregaming at the house earlier with Asya.

"I hope I was a good end of week closer for you." Callum touched my chin.

"Haven't had a closer this good in so long. Men don't slow dance anymore."

He laughed but I could tell he wasn't laughing at what I said, mostly because what I said wasn't a joke.

"What's funny?" I inquired.

"You sound like a professional dater. You're so used to being courted you can compare men across a spectrum to point out what the majority does and does not do. That's kind of funny to me."

"Your sense of humor is also unique." I made sure to let him feel his onlyness.

"I can't lie and say I don't like being one that doesn't fit your typical mold. I'm enjoying this island I am sitting on." His temperament was so controlled that it made me wonder how much he wasn't saying. I was intrigued.

"Now I'm curious about many things with you." I was honest.

"Likewise. But let's stay curious. For now, you know I like to slow dance and I know that you're actually very good at it. Even trade to me." His wit guided the conversation.

"Fair enough." I was pleased with his answer.

25

MAKING MOVES
Taya

"This product is trash. Why would we pick them up as a client?" I chimed into an already forming conversation.

"Yea the product is trash but it's an easy quick win for us. Lightweight tech work and we come up on a decent check." Asya and I sat in the boardroom on the third floor having our weekly team meeting with the other leads in our business, Sam, Gabrielle, and Felipe.

"If we know they're not a great product it could come back on us in the press," Gabrielle, our VP of Marketing, spoke up.

"If the press even cares. We'd have the job finished in a quarter and we could market quietly; a dark launch. In and out job," Sam, the VP of Engineering added. Felipe, from finance, nodded at the plan.

"Looks like it's three to two. Next order of business," Asya closed the topic.

After the meeting, I followed Asya up to her office. I had my weekly with Mike in a few and needed to grab her ear before she got busy. We took the stairs up to our floor. There are staircases on the south and north side of the building, with the purpose of safety exit options. But, Asya and I use the south stairs to move from meeting to meeting because the elevator is too high traffic and people try to distract us when we are too visible.

"Hope you don't mind me being at odds with you today," she started.

"Why would I? We're running a business, not a daycare." I honestly and truly didn't care that we have differing opinions, especially when it comes to tech release topics, that was Asya's area of expertise anyway. "I wanted to get your opinion on this venue for Mike." I switched the subject.

"You already got a venue?"

"Venue and line-up. Called a few of my old connections," I bragged.

"You mean you called some of your old hoes." She laughed while we walked past Shelly. I shot her a scowl but she didn't see me since she was walking in front of me. Once we got to the top floor we exited the stairwell and entered the fast-paced atmosphere that was our floor.

"Taya you got an 11 a.m. with Mr. Smell Good coming up," she yelled. I threw her a thumbs up and

Asya and I walked into her office and closed the door.

"Shelly is gon' hop on that man's dick one of these days for real." Asya laughed.

"I'm truly surprised it hasn't happened yet." And I was absolutely surprised. "Ok, check out these two venues." I showed her my iPad.

"Oh, this first one is sexy but the second one has more space."

"Exactly. I think we should go for scale because he has big numbers," I reasoned.

"Do you think you can pull off those kind of numbers?" She asked me a very real question. Something even I wasn't so sure about.

"We will see. Ok, and then if you swipe left a few more times those are the people I booked."

"Oh, bitch! Yes, I'm in that thang. It's bouta be a muthafucking movie." Asya validated I made good decisions.

I smiled. "Good that was the reaction I was looking for. I knew you would keep it a buck with me." I grabbed my iPad.

"Anyway, good luck with that new client of yours. Heard that business manager is a bitch."

"Now it's MY client? Oh, I thought you weren't salty bout it Taya." She stood and folded her arms looking at me hovering by her door.

"That was before you called my connects hoes." I faked an evil cackle leaving her office.

"PETTY!" she yelled from behind the closed

door.

"Hey, Taya" Shelly stopped me again. That was her thing, she had to say something to me every time I walked past. I never doubt if this woman is working because she always got an update for me every moment of the day.

"Yes, Shelly." I addressed her with eye contact this time.

"Michael is here a—"

"He's early. He'll have to wait," I interrupted, moving past her toward my office.

"Right but he wants me to ask you if you could do your hour over an early lunch. He has a flight he needs to catch in a few hours."

I huffed. "When's my next meeting?" I was looking for an excuse to say no.

"Not until 1:30." She already knew the answer. Something told me regardless of what my schedule was she was going to make it work for her favorite client.

"Fine let me grab my coat and my bag."

I thought he was up to something until I saw him in a Nike Tech Fleece like he was prepared for a long flight. He's usually, at minimum, business casual because his brand is all about impressing others but he clearly was dressed for utility. Everything he's been saying lately has all checked out. But, because of our history and my intuition for preventing bullshit, I wasn't planning on letting my guard down. The plan was and will remain to get this project finished and forever erase this man from my life. Even if that meant I had to play nice with him over an early lunch.

182

•••

"Thanks for being flexible with me." We sat down for lunch. I removed my coat and hung it on the back of the chair and placed my designer bag on the empty seat between us at the four-seater table.

"Where are you going anyway?"

"Cabo with my boys. A little real playas only trip." He clasped his hands together.

"Sounds like a thot trip." I halfway smiled.

"You know the vibes." His favorite narrative.

I rolled my eyes. "Would you like the update on your event?" I was back to business.

"Hell yea. What's up?"

"Ok, here's the place and the line-up." I handed him my iPad, showing him which direction to swipe. In the five minutes I had between getting Asya's opinion and getting my stuff to go to lunch, I rearranged the file images in an order that was presentable for a client.

He didn't say anything as he looked through the line-up.

"Well?" My curiosity was erupting.

"I like this spot. It's big. We can get a lot of sales up in there. But this line-up. Why you ain't ask me if you needed some better music connects?" I was insulted that he thought my connections weren't good enough.

"What's wrong with the ones here?"

"These sultry ass niggas? Where the hard rappers?"

I rolled my eyes. "What is a 'hard nigga' in the entertainment industry? Somebody that carries a gun or some shit? Or is it the rappers that always claim they only want the top?" I used air quotes to emphasize how stupid I thought that saying was.

"All these niggas look like somebody you probably let trick on you." He thought he was funny. He reminded me of Asya. Fuck both of them.

"You see yourself in there? Cause you definitely was tricking." I shot back because at this point I felt like I needed to defend myself.

He laughed. "True enough. Well, more niggas like me and less of these niggas." He somehow turned my insult into a fucking compliment. "I got you. I'ma make a few calls, baby don't worry bout it." He thought he was smooth.

"How about we keep my line up and add yours to a separate stage. Run two stages at once. One for the sultry and one for the hard." I put my professional hat back on. I also kinda liked the fluid idea and it made me think about how the show would appeal to a large audience this way thus, helping me pack out the show.

"I fuck with that idea heavy." He put my iPad down and went back to his meal. "You good at what you do, Miss Roberts." He pointed the end of his fork in my direction.

"I try. So next order of business, I hired a videographer for you. Whenever you're back from your thot trip, we'll get her to follow you around and get some footage for our media campaign. You know a lot of shots of you on your business shit. We'll need it because I'm setting up a traditional press conference right before the show starts and then the video can be used for anything after that."

"Send then with me to Cabo!"

"Mike. We need footage of you on your business shit, not you thot-locking and dropping." I expressed my concern with his change in my strategy.

"Nah show the people the real Money Mike."

"We're not promoting Money Mike. We're promoting Michael Keith."

"Yea but they the same nigga. I'm always on my Money Mike shit and my business shit. Ain't no separation."

I thought that was a dumb way to leverage his brands but he made valid points. I pulled out my phone and texted the videographer.

"You're covering the cost to fly her out," I added.

"No doubt. I'ma hit Taylor right now to get a flight and room for shorty." He pulled his phone out as well.

And just like that, we made moves. That was the best part about having Mike as a client, he's a fun. He doesn't need a real rigorous process to make shit happen, he has clout, money, and a lot of fucking natural confidence to get shit done.

Taya's Plight

186

26

LOS CABOS
Mike

"Her flight lands tomorrow. I've booked her in the same resort as you. I gave her your info to contact you when she's there," Taylor updated me on the videographer's travel arrangements.

"Cool. Oh, and before I forget I need you to get in contact with Taya's assistant–" I started.

"Shelly," Taylor added.

"Yea, her. Send her a list of some of our music connects. I'll let you pick but some make sure it's some popular mainstream rappers. Some of the hittas I bang on a consistent basis. Taya got this light-skinned pretty boy line-up and we need to add some fire to that hoe."

"You sure you want to interfere with Taya's vision? She knows her shit. Maybe a pretty boy line-up will bring out the fans," she added her two cents.

"True enough but at the end of the day, I'm promoting a studio. I need rappers and singers to pack out the session slots. Don't forget that I know my shit too," I reminded her.

"Understood. I'll get on that ASAP."

"Bet. Well, I'm bouta get loose with the boys in the meantime. Hit me if you need anything." I hung up.

After seven hours on a plane and an hour drive from the airport to the resort, I was finally in a position to be on my bullshit.

Dre, Lo, and our latest addition to the group, Vance had been in Cabo since earlier in the week. I told them I was gone have to join after a few days because I couldn't miss my meeting with Taya.

My niggas was happy to see me as soon as I stepped on the beach. They had a table out in the middle of our resort's bar area facing the ocean. I spent all of ten minutes in my room with a quick shower and threw on some swimming trunks and was ready to kick it.

"Bout time, nigga. Damn." Dre dapped me up on sight.

"Hell yea, late ass. Yo! Pour my man two Julio shots. He needs to catch the fuck up," Vance yelled over to the bartender. I could tell he was already lit.

Vance joined the group recently after we ran into him at the opening of a new sneaker boutique in the area. Turns out he owned the store.

"What you out in Oklahoma doing anyway, Mike," Lo jumped in.

"I'm in Texas. Nigga. Austin. Working on a marketing project for the new Atlanta stu."

"He out there working with Taya fine ass," Dre had to add.

"Taya. Damn. I ain't seen shorty in a minute. That's where she been?" Lo questioned.

"Yea she out there doing her thang."

"Who?" Vance was lost.

"Oh, nobody special. Just Money Mike's fine ass ex that he dragged through the mud then made her flee the city."

"Damn, Mike." Vance gave me a strong look.

"Nah, bro. That's not even how it went down. Just somebody I was fucking with for a minute."

"My G. You bought shorty an engagement ring." Dre was talking too fucking much.

"Word? I didn't even know that," Lo added.

I dropped my head in my hands. "Yo, where are those shots." I looked around for the waitress.

•••

The room was full of women. All kinds of bad bitches. Dre had one pinned across the sink in one of the bathroom. Lo was getting his dick sucked on the background and Vance was in the living area entertaining all the hoes.

I stumbled in after having too many shots on the beach.

"Money Mike come help me grab some off these lovely ladies," Vance slurred.

"Oh, this what you been on? I see you, bro. Let me get pretty mocha shawty in the white and slim baby in the red. Come here." I pointed and took two leaving Vance with three. I was all too used to pulling bitches outta line ups. This was a ritual for us.

The three of us went into my private room and shut the door.

"Look, ladies. I know I'm a fine ass smooth brotha but all I'm accepting tonight is neck and body kisses and head. Otherwise, y'all have fun with each other. I'm in a relationship." I let them know what was up but I also was too drunk to be working and stroking. That's why I fuck with threesomes; somebody is bound to be left out and I'm cool with it being me this time.

Pretty Mocha in the white went to work immediately. She glazed my dick in one swallow. She was talented. Before I knew it, I was passing out.

•••

I woke up with a mean ass headache. That tequila took ya boy smooth out. I completely forgot I had a threesome until I snatched the crust out my eyes and realized the two women from last night were still in my bed. Not to mention the videographer, a short lil blonde chick, was sitting on the guest loveseat in my room.

"Oh shit!" She caught me off guard. I looked down to make sure my dick was put away. At this point, anything could be out. "You must be the videographer," I spoke, not looking at her directly.

"Yep. Jude's the name." She followed my movements with her camera.

"You look like a Jude." That was mostly an insult but she didn't catch it.

"Thanks."

"How long have you been here?"

"Not that long. Just long enough to catch your crew escort a half a dozen women out. Looks like they forgot two." She pointed the camera in my bed.

"Yo chill on the footage, Judas." I shook Mocha and Slim to get them moving.

"Just Jude. I'm just tweaking the settings, figuring out how you move. Nothing major." She kept the camera rolling.

"Yea alright." I turned back to the ladies on my bed. "Say, y'all friends waiting for you outside," I lied in an attempt to get them to move quickly.

"Friends? I came here by myself. I don't even know her." Mocha pointed at Slim.

"Same." Slim grabbed her clothes.

I rubbed my hands forward across my head. "Well damn, I sholl couldn't tell last night. Anyway, I need y'all to go, no offense, ladies." The camera being in the room was making me paranoid.

I made Jude get out while I showered and gathered myself. My brain was pounding up against my forehead from all the tequila and I needed a fresh hot shower, some strong ass aspirin, and a shot to get me back right.

27

LOS CABOS, PART II
Mike

Day two in Cabo and I hadn't had a single drop of pussy despite what someone could think looking at Jude's footage. There was nothing about this place that made you want to work or focus. It was all about sun in the fun, a lot of tequila, and, when the sun went down, the nightlife.

We sat down to breakfast and Dre placed a bottle of Patrón on the table and asked the waitress for some orange juice.

"Mimosa's, mothafuckas!" He shouted soon as she walked off. I'm positive this fool hasn't been sober since he landed.

"Dre. You make mimosas with champagne not tequila, bro," Vance corrected this drunk fool.

"Shitttt, then we having Real-Playa-Mimosas. Turn the fuck up!" He slurred his words loudly and was adamant about his new drink so once the orange juice came back, we banged on Real-Playa-Mimosas for the rest of the morning. He said what he said.

"Last night was fucking crazy!" Lo managed to slip in a comment between chugs of drinks he was consuming.

"Man our room was swarming with hoes. At one point, I stopped counting and started admitting I didn't know any of their names," Dre jumped in.

"My boy, Mike came in late and didn't even attempt to ask nobody for a name. He gave them names based on outfits!" Vance screamed, getting the whole group to laugh. I looked over at Jude who was ducked off in the cut recording everything.

"Bro that's typical, Money Mike. This nigga can get any hoe and he don't even need to try. My man been bagging bitches. We shall call him Mr. Bitches." We hollered.

"Man chill out. I really calmed down a lot as of late. I lowkey got a shorty I'm trying to keep," I testified.

"Bruh? You cuffin?" Dre slurred.

"It's looking like that. I got a bad fine, grown, paid Black woman on her shit back in Miami waiting on me. Might officially lock that down when I get back in the city."

"Damn. That's big, Mike. Congrats, bro. She gotta be bad if you tryna call her wifey." Lo dapped me up.

"Fucking fine. Tall, coco, sexy ass woman." I thought about Dana. "Might have to drop Baby Money Mike off in that oven." Dre sat across from me with his mouth wide open. He literally couldn't believe what he was hearing. Hell. I couldn't believe I was saying it.

"Damn, Mike. I ain't know we were moving like this now, bro," Dre added.

"Now? Y'all niggas been fucking house this long? Y'all ain't had girlfriends yo whole twenties. We in our thirties now." Vance was surprised.

"Man. We have been on the same wavelength since we got out of high school," Lo added.

"Damn. Well for real congratulations, Mike. This some grown man shit you on." Vance was a well put together type of man. He had his fun but he had a wife and kids at the house that he took seriously. This nightlife shit was only a vacation thing and hearing us speak about it and finding out that we do this on a daily basis was shocking to him. I could see the sigh of relief on his face when he recognized that I was serious about coming out of the game. Hell, it wasn't until now that I realized I was serious about coming out of the game. But Vance was right, we was too fucking old to be fucking hoes and not learning their names.

"Rah rah rah! Fuck that. Let's get on some hoes. I don't have time for this Iyanla talk show shit," Dre started.

"My nigga, you funny. You don't like talking about anything other than women. What's that like? To be so childish?" Vance probably had two more Real-Playa-Mimosas than the rest of us and he was already the bold fearless type.

"Hoe, what you call me? Childish?" Dre stood up. The rest of us got up simultaneously, defensively.

"Nigga you heard me." Vance wasn't no soft ass either; he was with the shit.

"Whoa now. Everybody calm the fuck down." Lo put his hands out to signal everyone needed to take a step back. "Sit back down." He was taller and easily fifty pounds heavier than the rest of us so we generally listened when Lo got loud.

Dre shot Vance a mean look across the table and Vance didn't budge. Vance, through his body language, let it be known that if Dre wanted to throw hands then he was glad to get in the ring with him. But for the sake of our vacation continuing as planned, they agreed to disagree; Dre wanted to live his normal trifling life and Vance wanted acknowledgement for being a stand-up gentleman. In my opinion, both of these mothafuckas could say zero additional words for the rest of the trip and I was still going to have a good time. I didn't care and I for damn sure wasn't about to pick sides.

•••

That night we got it cracking at the club. Surprisingly, we survived unlimited Real-Playa-Mimosas, successfully woke up from a nap that we took on the beach, and managed to get fresh and dressed to go out. We had been drinking all day but we were all chugging

196

water bottles at the hotel suite to prepare for what we knew would be a wild ass night.

Jude was around for everything but she was so quiet I almost forgot that she was here with her video camera.

"My nigga got his shirt open with his chest out. Alright, I see you," Lo yelled across the room at Vance.

"You watching my fit kinda close, my nigga," he shot back but we all knew that was a compliment outta love. That's how we do; show love through indirect half-ass jokes. It is the American Black Man way.

I wore a navy slim fitted casual suit. Black button-down underneath, no tie. Threw on some cologne and brushed my hair right before we took off to our car service. We all looked good in our complimentary attire. Vance was on his Miami Vice shit, chest out. Dre and I had similar styles and Lo was rocking a silky button-down with a brimmed hat like he was about to pose for a trendy magazine. What we were wearing didn't really matter, all four of us knew that by the end of the night we would have a story to tell.

The club was thick. We pulled up a little after midnight and beelined to the entrance from our car. It was no need to stand in line because I was there. I pulled the Money Mike card way before I arrived in Mexico by having Taylor work with our public relations crew to let it be known that I would be vacationing here. They were waiting for me.

"Mr. Keith," the general manager, Marisol,

reached for my hand soon after I passed the threshold of the establishment. "We have prepared a section for you and your guests." She pointed to a corner. She was a little over five foot six, well dressed with a Spanish accent. Not too bad to be looking at. I glanced over at the section she pointed out to me.

"Why a section away from the party?" I was still holding her hand as I leaned in to speak in her ear.

"Oh, I just assumed you'd like something more private. I have other options available if you'd like to choose." She waved her free hand around the room to showcase that there were a few other available sections. I looked back at my boys.

Dre nodded in the direction of the section he had his eyes on. I understood his gesture.

"We'll take that one and one bottle of your finest tequila, cognac, and champagne. And please send your best bottle girls."

She smiled and then went off to make it happen. She already knew I had the funds to pay for whatever I was asking for so she didn't even bother showing me the bill before seating us and sending over my bottle request.

Marisol gave me her card and told me to ring her if I needed anything and then she faded off into the crowd to run her club.

The spot we were at was a mix of Spanish and hip-hop vibes and the women in attendance matched that swag as well.

Dre bagged ninety percent of the women sitting in our section and none of us minded because he had good taste.

Some mixed shorty, you know the type: light-skinned with wavy hair, stood up on the couch in her tight fitted spandex dress that stopped right below her cheeks and started twerking until her dress rose up, exposing her entire ass. At this point, everybody was drunk off their ass and fascinated with the bare ass that was moving. Feeling challenged, the chick next to her pulled her top over her head exposing her bare large titties. It wasn't my style to let bare titties go unsucked, so I grabbed shorty, sat her in my lap, and started motorboating. In hindsight, I would have appreciated the table Marisol offered us now that it was getting heated in our very exposed section. Dre was getting danced on by shorty that exposed her naked ass to us. A very nice ass, might I add. Lo was entertained by a few and Vance had made his way to the dance where we held a champagne bottle over his head while he rapped the lyrics to Lil Wayne's version of "Watch My Shoes."

"...*back in this bitch but a lot more rich on my Papa Bear shit, need hot porridge, gotta lot more shit than you could ever fathom, a big head nigga couldn't even imagine...*"

He held the champagne bottle like an imaginary microphone and was going in, having the time of his life. Meanwhile, the rest of us were about one piece of clothing away from getting some pussy in the club. Matter of fact, Dre was already there, getting rode on by the naked ass girl. He got off quite a few strokes before security came through dragging all the naked hoes from our section.

Dre fought for them to stay like they were people he actually knew. All while I gave no fucks and sat back finishing my drink. Dre followed the security guard, yelling at dude to let the one he was fucking go. Finally, the guard got tired of his shit and yelled back, "She's sixteen! She shouldn't even be in here."

All three of us sat there with our mouths wide open. Dre was getting his dick waxed by a sixteen-year-old girl in public and I couldn't help but think about how old the girl was whose whole ass titties were just in my mouth.

"Let's go!" Dre was pissed and clearly starting to sober up after realizing what he had done. None of us moved. "Man, LET'S FUCKING GO!" He screamed over the music.

I heard him the first time but I was still thinking through the whole scenario. I downed my drink then put my suit jacket back on and followed behind the pack. We flagged Vance down. He was drenched in sweat from hosting his private concert that nobody asked for.

"What's up, man? I'm just getting started." He wasn't ready to leave.

"Nah we gotta get ghost, bro." I pulled him closer and told him. Trying not to let Dre hear me. Vance was a smart man, so he heard me without further explanation, handed the half full bottle of expensive champagne to the first woman he saw then followed us out the club and into the car.

"Somebody tell me what happened?" Vance

demanded after we packed into our host car. The driver took off toward our resort.

Nobody said anything at first. Vance was confused.

"Them girls in our section…" Lo started.

"Were wild as fuck. Got ass naked off the strength. The brown-skinned one had some big ass titties…" He referred to the girl I was messing with.

"Yea. Them. They were underaged," Lo finished.

"Shit eighteen and nineteen-year-olds stay in them twenty-one and up clubs. Y'all know how it be." He was casual about the situation. It got quiet again for just a second, then he realized it was deeper than that. "Younger?" He followed up.

"Sixteen, bro," I answered finally.

He sat there with the exact same expression we all had. I didn't even mention that Dre was fucking one of them. We actually never brought it up. We crashed for the night and then the next morning, we took our flights back into the states.

28

TEMPORARY SITUATION
Mike

I had been at least five weeks since I was back at my crib which meant it has been exactly five weeks too long for *my girl* to go without seeing me.

After my extended weekend bro-cation, I needed to clear my mind and get back right. I was lucky enough to have a plane ride directly back to Miami that none of my boys were on. I wasn't trying to revisit or do any recaps from the prior days. I had decided it was best to just drop those events in the vault under "shit that happened but didn't happen" and move forward.

After the flight, I made my way to my car that Taylor graciously dropped off at the airport for me earlier that day after I told her I'd rather she not pick me up. I made a quick stop by the crib for a shower, shave, and a fresh look. Had to make sure I was on my shit; looking, smelling, and feeling good. Then, I drove the Benz out to Dana's side of town. It was late, just past two am, but I wasn't worried about that. I was planning to wake her up anyway, quite physically. We had a few conversations over the past couple weeks where she directly expressed that she wished I was around during the night. I figured I'd make her dreams come true and pop up as a gift.

She owned a three bedroom, three bath situation in a ducked off neighborhood. I pulled into her driveway and switched the car off. Her two-car garage was closed and that's where I was assuming her car was tucked away. The house was dim. Her neighborhood is one of those places that would be labeled as a "good area;" nothing like where my house was located in the deep suburbs but she had a good location. She had a lot of yard space, a very family-like home for a solo type of woman. I had only picked Dana up from her house and not been in it but I figured I could park in her driveway; it was late and I would leave before she was planning to head out for the day.

I hopped out. Situated my manhood in my joggers and approached the house. The porch light came on as soon as I hit the brick walkway. I looked around just to check my surroundings and make sure nobody was watching me.

I pounded the side of my fist against the wood. Waited for a minute then I rang the doorbell. Waited two minutes. It was too breezy outside to be waiting this long, so I called her.

She picked up on the first ring.

"Mike is that you out outside?" She was whispering.

"Yea, what's up with you not opening the door?" I was pissed.

"Why are you here?" She whispered and then hung up before opening the door just enough to fit her body through. She slid out, joining me on the porch.

"What the fuck is wrong with you?" I yelled.

"Can you calm down?" She continued to whisper.

"What?" I yelled again. I was pissed she was still whispering and, more importantly, because I was wondering why she wasn't welcoming me into her home with open arms.

"My husband is sleeping and he'll hear you if you keep yelling!" She still whispered but at a slightly louder tone as she pulled me by my arm trying to drag me back to the car. She.

"Husband?!" I was shocked and most definitely not whispering like her. Fuck her and her husband.

The next sound I heard was the barrel of a shotgun being cocked. DOOM! Double bullets flew past me into the front yard. I pushed Dana and ran toward my car. I struggled to push the unlock button for one second then I hopped in and skurrrrted off! Before I could get away from her house another shot let off. This time, a bullet hit my back window, shattering the glass. I ducked as I pressed the down on the gas leaving a cloud of burned rubber on the residential street behind me.

•••

"She did what now?"

Taylor was the first person I told the story to on the next day.

"She came outside whispering about a husband and the next thing I know my back window is shot out." I was stretched out in my desk chair, reclining with my feet up. She sat across the way from me on the edge of my desk like she normally does.

She laughed.

"Taylor. Really? This shit funny to you?" I pulled my phone out to call Dre.

"Wait. What are you doing?" She was still halfway laughing, leaning over trying to grab my phone. I defended against the action.

"I'm calling my boys. We pulling up on dude for the damage to my Benz."

"Michael, that man didn't do anything you wouldn't have done. You were in a relationship with his wife."

"She never told me she was married. I done fucked inside the bedroom and everything." I put my phone down.

206

"There's no doubt that she is trifling as hell but still you were smashing his wife. Look at it from his perspective. You lucky to be alive right now. Based on the story you just told me, if dude had just a little bit better aim you would be dead." She wasn't wrong.

"Man, whatever. See, this is exactly why men dog women. Look at this shit." I was hot.

"Please. You get one trifling hoe and decide to write them all off. You are attracted to all the wrong women. You ignore all the great women standing right in your face." She didn't make eye contact on that last statement. Instead, she got up and made her way back to her desk outside my office.

29

THAT SNATCH
Taya

He picked me up and wrapped my legs around him. He used his hands so much. With so much confidence. He took his time. He wanted to feel everything. He made use of his lips placing them gently across the nape of my neck. Slow, long motions followed by a smack. Slow. Long. Smack. My mouth was wide open. My eyes closed. My body relaxed. I exhaled, trying to reclaim my breath.

He paused, looked at me attentively in my eyes, and followed with a soft bottom lip only kiss, and then he paused again. My whole body was warm and engaged. He pulled my dress over my head and then laid me across his bed. My entire body was arched; my legs at a soft angle, my titties upright, my nipples pointed toward the ceiling, my ass touching the sheets meanwhile my lower back was suspended. He pulled his shirt over his head, exposing his body, and slid his joggers off then he crawled on to the bed next to me.

Laying his head on the pillow, he finally spoke, "You have great lips."

I sucked my bottom lip. "Yours are better," he smiled. He ran his pointer finger over my right nipple, the one closest to his body.

With confidence, he glided his palms across both my breasts to tease me. Moving them back and forth a few times until they were firm and hard. He smiled, watching me react, and, when he was satisfied, he moved me back into the comfort of his hold. We wrapped our lips around each other once more as I ran my fingers across the back of his neck. In the midst of our passion, I touched his ears with the tip of my fingers.

"Don't do that," he moaned between our kisses, or at least that's what I thought he said because his expression of how good he felt was louder than his actual words. I could tell my mere presence made him erect and the soft feels between my nipples and my fingers had him anxious.

"Say it again..." I commanded gently with my voice, still caught up in our passionate lip exchange.

He came up for air with more clarity in his voice. "Don't do that. That's my spot. Don't play."

"Oh…" I said, grabbing the back of his neck

and pulling him closer.

I changed my attention to his left ear, licking the perimeter of his lobe. Because, of course, when somebody tells you not to touch their spot that's a direct signal to go crazy. He lost all composure as the tension built up. He couldn't even focus on kissing me anymore. These ears of his were indeed his spot.

His fingers pressed against my cheeks while he repressed his moans but I could tell he was screaming my name inside his head. I made it my job to softly but aggressively press my lips against every inch of his neck, ears, and chest.

Callum grabbed me and moved me off his neck, probably so that he could take a moment to breathe but to also place me in the position he wanted me in first. With incredible skill, he pinned me against his warm silk sheets, moved my legs apart from each other, and slid his long ass bare dick inside me. He was so long he touched the back of my pussy on the first stroke. I moaned on entry, lifting my back as a reflex. But, he fixed that immediately, pulling back just enough on the next stroke to make me comfortable. He could read body signals like nobody's business. He paid attention to everything I did and either adjusted or continued based on his assessment. And he was spot on every time.

Because he had a lot of dick, his strokes were paced. Long controlled strokes until he had all my juices flowing then he switched to faster shorter strokes leaving most of his manhood inside of me. I ripped the pillow behind me with my left hand.

"Talk to me," he demanded. This wasn't a question rather a direct demand to tell him how good he already knew he was.

"Tell me this is mine," again he demanded.

"Yes, Daddy, it's yours." I could barely speak but I followed his command.

"Say it again."

"It's yours." I placed my hand on his chest trying to create separation between us because he was tearing my shit up.

He threw my hand back and then pinned my hands against the bed.

"Say it louder." He stared at me directly in my eyes.

"It's yours, Daddy!" I screamed as he took me to my first climax. I moaned and came all at the same time. He stroked through my wetness continuing the sensation as long as my pretty pussy would allow it.

When he could tell I was done he pulled out and laid next to me.

"Suck my dick. Make me cum," he said in this sexy ass sultry voice. I followed his direction. He was so demanding in the bedroom and that shit was turning me on.

I wanted to return the favor so I did what I had to do. I fit most of his dick into the back of my throat and started to move my mouth across his length. He used his right hand and thrust himself just a little bit further into my throat, pushing the bounds of my head game. He had his left hand rested behind his head with his eyes closed.

"Snatch my soul." He was serious.

I tightened the grip of my mouth around his dick and I bobbed and slobbed all over his manhood. Spit slid down to his balls and I made it my job to lick that off as well. Just as I was getting into it, he pulled himself out, threw me on my back, grabbed both my titties with his hands, and slid his dick between them until he covered my whole chest in creamy cum. He threw his head back as he finished.

Enough days had passed since the last time I was with Callum. He was the first person I thought about in the morning and stayed on my mind the entire day. The moment he invited me over to his house for a glass of wine was the moment I realized I really liked him. That wine turned into some fire ass toe curling sex and, what frightened me the most, was having strong feelings for him.

•••

After we showered, he held me in his arms in his bed.

"You sleep?" I asked him, not moving.

"Not yet, what's up?"

"You are so good at that," I admitted.

"At what?"

"Sex."

He laughed. "Had a lot of practice." He kissed

my forehead.

"You're supposed to tell me the same thing." I was fishing for compliments.

"I didn't think I needed to say it. It's hard not to come with you on the first ten strokes. You got that snatch." He laughed. I was relieved. I really felt like his sex game made mine look like trash and I'm a beast in these sheets. He caught me off guard. But I found peace in his answer and went back to silence snuggled up under him.

30

LOVE DON'T LIVE HERE
Mike

"Mike are you fucking serious?!" Taya raised her voice during our weekly sync. This was the first sync after my brief hiatus to Cabo and my very very quick detour back to Miami.

She was reviewing the footage that Jude sent to her. I specifically requested to Jude that she should share it with me first but she bypassed my ask and shipped it directly to Taya's office. I had no chance to prepare and, quite frankly, I wasn't sure if Taya was looking at me clapping some cheeks or chopping it up with my boys. I was basically speechless sitting across from her.

"So, you're just not going to say anything, huh?"

"I don't know what you are referring to." I

leaned back clearly taking the oblivious route.

"Mike. Please. You know what you were on in Cabo. There's nothing but liquor, women, and sex in this footage. Oh, oh, and let's not glaze over this casual cocaine usage. These girls are snorting drugs off of your abs. You forgot that happened?" She continued to browse, gazing into her computer screen with a look of disdain. I had actually forgotten that cocaine thing happened.

"Look. I was turnt up with my boys. It happens." I defended myself.

"Michael, what do you suggest I do with this raunchy ass footage? Because though I think this gets you clout with the younger audience, this immediately puts you in the not-at-all-serious businessman category that clearly your Black ass deserves to be in." She was mad.

"Fine. We don't use the footage. Who gives a fuck?"

"I give a fuck. I already have your press run lined up and need to ship media assets over to the distributing companies in a few days. Did you forget this is a public relations initiative? Did you forget you asked me to pack out a fifty studio building in the first week of sales? Or are you brain dead from all the tequila?" I could tell those were rhetorical questions.

I dropped my head into my hands trying to create some space to think. "Yea, that's right." I followed.

"So, Mr. Let Them See The Real Money Mike, what do you suggest we do? Because if I run this footage I can pretty much kiss my polished PR record goodbye, not to mention your ass don't make nearly half the money you were expecting. And trust, my fee percentage has not changed. You will run me my cash regardless." She was fierce.

"Look. I fucked up. I got carried away with my boys and had a good time. Don't run the footage but really it's your job to figure out what we do about this media run. I'll be available to shoot more polished content, just let me know what you come up with. I got shit to do and I don't really like how you're talking to me right now. So, with all due respect, you figure this shit out." I made my final words then I exited her office.

I walked out the double glass doors from her office, past Shelly's desk, and toward the elevator.

"See you next week, Mr. Keith." Shelly always had to say something to me.

"Bet." I hit her with a hand gesture then stepped into the elevator.

Once I got to the first floor, I ran right into some badass thing. Ever since Dana played me like a bitch I was back on my fuck boy shit. Money Mike in full effect.

"I got these same Gucci links." I pointed out the accent pieces on her suit. Well dressed and bad. She was definitely up my alley.

She looked up at me and smiled. I could tell she was thinking. Then, she folded her arms and responded.

"Yep. Gucci does what has to be done with these suits." She was for sure confident about what she was presenting. I was focused on bagging.

"Look, I'm about to grab lunch. You should join me. Let me spend some cash on you and get a good conversation going." I was smooth.

She laughed. Then, she extended her hand. "I'm Asya. Co-owner of this business you're standing in. Pretty sure you're familiar with my business partner. As an owner here you could imagine I'm way too familiar with our clients. It's a pleasure to have met you, Mike. Enjoy your lunch." She shook my hand and then walked away. She didn't even give me a chance to try to lie.

•••

Later that night, I almost cleared out a whole bottle of cognac. I couldn't believe where my life was heading. I used to be the type of man that nobody told me no and now I'm getting cheating on, lied to, told what to do, and, the most devastating of all, rejected by women. I didn't have enough context to realize I was flirting with a woman that is the business partner of my ex. What kind of sloppy ass mothafucka was I turning into?

•••

My mom held down a little ass one bedroom apartment on the west side of this country ass little city in rural Georgia. We didn't have much of shit. I was lucky to have more than one meal a day because shit was tight around my house. I was the only child to my mother but one of many to my father. My pops had so many kids I never figured out how many real siblings I had. My mom had this badass habit of getting attached to ain't shit as men and trying to make space for them in our already tiny ass apartment. I had so many uncles it was embarrassing.

On this particular morning, I remember it like it happened to me yesterday, I woke up on my make-do pallet of blankets that lay in the corner of our living room, that was my room, I heard my mom arguing, yelling at somebody. Naturally, I assumed she was getting into it with her latest boyfriend and tried to ignore it while making a dry bowl of cereal. Her loud remarks were followed by a man's voice. Just like I thought she was arguing with a man. Same shit different day. That was until I heard a loud thump like something fell over.

At the time I was nine but I was smart enough to know when shit was going bad. I walked down the narrow hallway that led to the only bedroom in the apartment and placed my ear against the door. I heard my mother crying, begging. I didn't know what to do, I didn't even know who else was in the room. In the following seconds, her screams grew; the sound of her shrills made my skin crawl. Before I could decide what to do the door flung open and the man in the room fled holding a bloody knife. I pushed the door back to see my mother lying on the floor in a pool of her own blood with fluids gushing from her neck as she grabbed for me. With the last bit of energy she had left she whispered, "Help." Seconds later she died.

My mother was never nice to me, nor did she give me anything other than the space she let me use to sleep on our living room floor. She always put any and everybody else before me. She *didn't care if I went to school or how I got there. And, from what she would yell at me on many occasions, she blamed her life's misfortune on my father. In those first few seconds after her death I was relieved. I never cried.*

The police showed up to the apartment shortly after I called the authorities and after questioning me for a few days, I was shipped to a foster unit. I spent the next seven years of my life with the same lackluster parenting that my own mother offered me. I had foster mothers that abused me, yelled, lied, and stole, and some that were milder but really could care less about me. To me, it was all the same; no woman had ever loved me and I wasn't expecting it from anyone.

31

QUIET BACKGROUND DEALS
Taya

"I need your professional advice," I admitted to Winsdale. This was my first time asking her for anything job-related and it had to have been at least five years since I was stumped by a client.

"Sure. That's literally why I'm here." I followed her into her finely decorated office.

"Have a seat. Let's talk. How's Mr. Keith?" She started the conversation.

"That's what I need your advice on." I took a seat in one of the plush chairs opposite her.

"I'm listening."

"So here's the short version: his company's game-changing press run is scheduled and ready. We're planning to run content on some of the south's biggest platforms. The best media coverage money can buy—"

221

"Perfect. Sounds like this project is closing nicely," Catherine cut me off.

"Right, except, I got his media footage back and, quite frankly, its hours and hours of incriminating footage nothing that we could safely brand and run." I was honest.

"Incriminating?" She focused in on that particular part. She had her thinking face on.

"Seriously illegal shit. I mean … minus the illegal footage, everything else is basically trash reality tv footage. I have no time to get new footage and good editing and I already promised video reel to some distributor partners that respect me as a PR professional. I need a new angle. That's the advice I need from you." I put it all on the table.

"Hmm…" she thought for a second. "Shut It Down could go up in flames if you released this content."

"Right, which is why I'm planning not to. But I need something to get out there."

"Well, let's think about this. We drop content implicating illicit activities of Mr. Keith. He goes under public scrutiny, possibly face legal investigations. Question… was he aware the cameras were present?"

"Aware?! He insisted I send the videographer with him on his trip." I remembered the day we made that deal.

"Then, technically, under our PR contractual agreement, you have fulfilled the duties of a diligent agent. Thus, the business could receive no backlash from this press run. We'd need to make sure we covered our publishing tracks. Would hate to have your name on something so cynical, with a background like yours that would stick out like a sore thumb on your resume."

"Where are you going with this?" I was confused.

"Release the footage. Proceed with the press run. CYA but fulfill the terms of our contract."

"Catherine, that would ruin Michael. Maybe he keeps some of his sales because he's customers don't care but his goals of advancing in that industry die the moment I release that media." I was empathic.

"So? Not your problem. Plus, Shut It Down would be exposed and who better than the female badass mogul who happens to be in a position to grab it." She sat back, taking a sip from her mug.

I thought about it for a second. I could ruin Mike and acquire Shut It Down. I have the capital for it and would make a nice expansion to our tech startup. Our business had the software and engineers that studios could benefit from and owning the studios too would be a bonus. I could triple my income with one press run. And after all the shit Mike did to me last year, I owe his ass.

"Taya you could have his whole business. Shut It Down could be yours."

"And what do you get?" I was curious why she was so invested in this proposition.

"Well. I get one less competitor in Atlanta. I've

been working to figure out how I could keep Mr. Keith close in order to at least get a cut of his new income. And more importantly, a very successful friend who owns a pair of studios." She was honest.

Catherine Winsdale wasn't successful on accident. She made some of the most high powered, but silent moves I've ever witnessed in this business. But, one thing about these type of people is that they have no loyalty; had it been me in Mike's position she'd advise someone to snatch everything from under me.

"Let me sleep on it. I'll let you know how I move in a few days." I closed the conversation.

"Looking forward to hearing what you come up with." She smiled. We shook and then I took off.

32

I Need a Favor
Taya

"She told you to throw that man to the wolves?" Asya asked over our usual wine and dinner series at the house.

"Girl. Gave me the exact blueprint to ruining this man's life." I confirmed.

"Well…" she started then paused.

"Well, what?"

"He is a shady ass man. He don't give a fuck about nobody. Did I tell you he actually tried to run game on me in the lobby of our building?" She confessed.

"What?" I raised my eyebrows.

"Yes. He complimented my Gucci suit. You know the cute fitted tan one I wore the other day for my meeting with the French gentlemen from NetCore? I looked good in that suit, even Guillaume was checking me out–" She was flattering herself at this point.

"Asya…" I interrupted.

"My bad. Anyway, yea. he walked up on me and offered me lunch like he just knew I was about to take it. First off, bitch, I'm busy, you know with running a business. Clearly, he didn't think I was wearing that expensive ass suit to be answering phones at the front desk. I spent a whole twelve seconds professionally curving him and reminding him I was the business partner of yours. We probably should call facilities to see if they finished mopping up his face off the lobby floor, cause BAY-BAY I gathered his ass." She was so expressive.

I shook my head. "Honestly I'm not surprised. You should watch the footage I have of him in Cabo. I can't believe I was really contemplating being with that man permanently. He is trifling with women, treating them like they are an activity rather than people. But I will say one of his friends, I think his name is Vance, was the only gentlemen out the bunch. The rest of them were straight disgusting."

"Hmm, do you know if he's single?" Asya looked interested.

"Have no clue. Oh, you must have removed ol' boy from the roster, what's up with you and Todd? I doubt he'd want you looking into all these new interests you seem to be paying attention to." I reminded her.

"Oh, Todd is misbehaving. I told him he was getting too comfortable with this pussy and told him he could return after he thought about his actions." She laughed. I did too.

"But on to more pressing news, bitch are you fucking Callum?" She was all up in my business.

I laughed. "Oh my god! That man. Whew."

"Wait. Light skinned, power drill, never-had-the-hoes Callum got it like that?" Asya had me weak.

"When I say that man is blessed. He snatched the shit out of my soul. And, look, I don't even want it back. He can keep it. His entire presence, in general, is a mood. Not only is his sex hardcore fire, he is also smart, can hold an amazing conversation, teaches me shit that I never knew, is into me beyond my physical, and is all-around dope."

"Honestly I can't say I'm surprised. Callum is a good guy. I was just expecting his sex to be boring."

"Hell nah. Far from boring. He beat it and put me to sleep. I only fucked him once and I'm hooked. I'm trying to be his girl but I don't want to scare him off."

"If there's anything I've learned about grown men it's that you gotta say what you want. They can't read minds at all."

"True enough," I agreed.

"And what about Rashad? Or Brandon?"

I sighed, picking up my oversized wine glass. "For the last time, Brandon and I are not a thing. I gave him a few rounds of this pussy, that's it. That's all. Rashad… I haven't talked to him in months. Guess we're officially done." I didn't lie, I hadn't given him a thought in months and he stopped trying to reach me a long time ago. I guess he finally got the hint.

"That's what I thought. If only you could change the narrative and reprogram these niggas. At least enough that you could fool yourself into thinking they are good people." She shook her head.

My mind wandered for a second; I was having an epiphany.

"Oh shit. I think I got it." I stood up quickly.

"Got what?!" Asya stood up too.

"I got the idea, how we can fix Mike's campaign run. I gotta go to the office and make some last minute calls. Don't wait up for me." I grabbed my coat and my keys and downed my drink before heading out of the house.

"Hey, Brandon," I made a phone call as soon as I got into the car. "I need a legal favor, a cover my ass big time favor. You got me?"

I had an idea that I was ninety-five percent sure was going to work but I also had a few other dependencies I needed to think through, Winsdale in particular. Talking with Asya reminded me why I wanted to secure Brandon as a contact in the first place.

33

Courtesy Link Up
Taya

I met Rashad at this little spot out east, past all the shopping centers. Texas is good for taking your money via an outlet or a shopping center. But, today, I wasn't focused on shopping. I had unfinished business with Rashad and I needed to close that chapter respectively. I figured it had been long enough and we could revisit the conversation that we left open the night I walked out of his crib. He had made just enough attempts to contact me that I knew there were some things he wanted to get off his chest. Since I was focused on moving forward with Callum, I didn't see why I needed to allow this topic to stay open any longer. The more time passed, the more I realized how much of a rebound Rashad was for me after Mike.

Last night, I sent Rashad a vague text requesting he meet me. At first the "waiting as they write" bubbles appeared, and then they disappeared and reappeared as if he was contemplating what to send me. Then, he responded, simply "Bet. I'll be there."

I could tell he was treating this as his last attempt just by what he was wearing and how he smelled. He was wearing that expensive soft cologne that he knows I cannot resist and had, on many occasions, tore him out of his clothes just to get a sniff. He wasn't slick. What he was was fine. His hair was freshly faded and his beard lined and moisturized.

"It's been a minute," I awkwardly started the conversation.

I was sporting a simple look. Grey leggings, white cropped shirt, oversized dark tinted shades that I pulled off my eyes, and a slick ponytail. I was wearing no make-up, just fresh skin, glossed lips, and huge hooped earrings.

"Yea I saw Mike out here a few months back. I guessed that was why you ain't feel the need to get back to me." He sipped his drink looking off. He slipped that in and I could tell he wanted me to address it.

"It's true. Mike has been around. But on strictly business terms. Nothing romantic, I assure you." I motioned with my hands to drive my point.

"Yea he told me it was on some business shit but I know how good ol Money Mike can be."

"Excuse me. You think I can't control my actions based on the presence of a man? I feel like that's really hypocritical coming from you." I folded my arms.

He looked me in my face for the first time. "I didn't mean it like that. I just mean that I know what kind of person Mike can be." He wasn't helping his case.

"I'm well versed in that subject and know how to handle myself. But that's not why I came here to talk to you."

"What are you trying to be my girl again?" He smiled.

"No." I was direct. His expression changed. "I wanted you to know that I moved on."

"Damn and here I was waiting for you to give me a chance to make it up to you. I thought we had something real. You moved on kind of fast, don't you think?" He wasn't happy and was trying to keep his composure.

"Rashad, that's not fair." It wasn't.

"I understand that what I did wasn't ideal but I just thought we were better than that." He was reaching now.

"We were. But, let's not forget it was you that cheated. I reserve all the rights to decide if I want to give you a second chance or not. I've been dumb in past relationships and done the whole second chance thing just to later learn that I can't actually forget what happened."

"I feel like I made it easy for you to cop out because it's clear you were just using me as a rebound. and this little ass cheat was a good excuse to get rid of your rebounder." He went up an octave.

"Now you know that's bullshit."

"Is it? Because I do recall me and you being a thing only a few weeks after your heart got shattered by ya boy."

"What kind of dumb ass female do you think I am to let a "rebounder," as you say, uproot my life in Miami and move me out here? That's a bit much for a rebound. I was into your ass. Extremely invested in case you forgot. And what in the fuck is a little cheat? You had sex with a different woman while in a relationship with me. You cheated and I don't have to accept that shit. And you are lucky I'm doing this courtesy link up because I could have just continued to leave your ungrateful ass on read." I put my shades back over my eyes and stood up. Rashad stood too, grabbing me by my arm.

"Wait. Wait. Stop." He motioned me to sit back down. In my mind, this conversation was going nowhere and I didn't need the interrogation. However, I did want to be done with this shit, so I sucked it up and sat back down with my arms folded. "I'm sorry. You're right. I... I really did think I would get a second chance with you and this is just heartbreaking for me. I fucked up. That's on me." Rashad finally offered a sincere apology.

We paused for a second and let the energy around us rebalance after those heated exchanges.

"Look, I haven't always just been the most perfect person myself and somehow the universe keeps allowing me to start over. I wish you nothing but the best, honestly." I meant every word of that.

Rashad grabbed both of my hands, raised the right one, and gently placed his lips against the back of it. I accepted this sincere gesture as his surrender as he released our once fiery and unstoppable, internal connection.

34

ALL THE WRONG ONES
Mike

"Michael, I have been calling you nonstop all day." Taylor used her spare key to get into my house and forced my curtains open, filling my room with the sun for the first time in days.

"I'm taking a few days off," I groaned, sitting myself up in bed.

"It's been a week. You don't need any more days off. Your Atlanta reveal is this weekend, you need to be prepped and ready. I've given you all the time I could." She rambled through my room picking up clothes and clearing clutter.

"This weekend?" It had slipped my mind.

"This weekend. Taya called and said she couldn't get in contact with you a few days ago. She's releasing your media run soon and then she's flying into Atlanta to meet us for the event. We need to get you together. You need a haircut, a fresh shave, and to soak in someone's bathtub." She held her nose after pulling my comforter back and realizing I wasn't as fresh as I normally am.

"I don't think I can do this." I got back under the covers.

"What is going on with you?" She sat on the edge of the bed looking directly in my face. "We've worked so hard for this and we're so close. Why are you giving up?"

Truth was, I didn't care anymore. I couldn't recall where I made a wrong turn but it was extremely clear to me that I had made one somewhere along the line. I wasn't really the nigga that I thought I was. Here I am a wealthy good-looking thirty-year-old and I couldn't get a woman to take me seriously if I paid her. My legacy was about to stop with me; all the hard work I put in was only short lived.

"Look. I get it. Things have gotten really hard for you lately. I can see it's wearing you down. But, I cannot allow you to stop here. You'd never forgive yourself."

"Yea, I know." Is all I had to offer to this conversation. I forced myself to get up and attempted to restore myself. Luckily I could always fall back on my good looks, even when I felt like shit. Regardless of how I was feeling, Taylor was right. We had a plan we'd been working on for months and I needed to finish this shit.

We caught our flight into Atlanta right on time and enjoyed the luxury that first-class had to offer all the way in. Taylor briefed me on everything that I missed. Where I needed to be on the day of the event, what I needed to say, and everything else Taya had planned. Taylor seems unconcerned about what her plan was but I was lowkey nervous, I'm not gone lie. Last time I chopped it up with Taya I basically told her she needed to clean up a mess that I started. And I ain't heard nothing from her since then. But, according to Taylor they been in contact daily and everything was set to take off. At this point, I just had to trust the process and see what was going to shake.

When we landed in Atlanta, we grabbed a fresh luxury rental whip for the weekend and headed down to the venue. Taylor needed to confirm for Taya that everything was set up according to her layout. Taya wasn't planning to fly in until the day of. Instead, she sent Shelly to collaborate with Taylor on all the little details.

"There he goes! Mr. Smell Good himself. Mmm. Looking just like your normal self might I say. Yes Lord," Shelly greeted us. Taylor thought the whole thing was funny. I wasn't laughing.

"Finally nice to meet you in person, Miss Taylor. Little slim fine thang you are as well." They embraced.

"The pleasure is absolutely all mine, Shelly. How's everything so far?" Taylor jumped right into it. Shelly was still eyeballing me but turned her attention to

Taylor's question.

"Everything is happening. The production crew has been here since early this morning putting everything together. We have the two stages that need to be fully set up on each end of the venue, the green rooms are being prepped in the back, the logistics team is in the back as well working through all the RSVPs and working out the kinks in the check-in process for our guests. Taya is back in Austin with a jammed packed agenda connecting with each and every performer, making sure everything is good to go. Sis hasn't slept all week. Baby has been working. She'll be arriving a few hours before the event starts. You know Taya, she has to make an entrance." Shelly gave us all the details.

I did know Taya and that was a fact, she absolutely had to make an entrance, even on her worst days, she showed up in full form.

"Anything we can do to help?" Taylor asked, checking her own list.

"As long as, Mr. Star of the Show is prepped and ready for his intro speech then we are all covered."

"He's ready," Taylor answered, looking over to me to confirm.

"Yea, I'm ready. This is the type of shit I do. No big deal."

"No big deal? Twenty thousand RSVPs and that's not including the talent and their entourages. Whew. Y'all are built differently because I would be shitting a brick if I needed to get on that mic," Shelly laughed.

"I was built for this. I'm all good." I was finding my confidence again, remembering that Money Mike ain't just my name.

That night, after dinner, we checked into our suite. Taylor and I figured it was easier to share the same space since we need to be in sync for the event and we were only going to in town for forty-eight hours.

"So you never gave me an update on Dana."

Taylor broke the silence that was in the living room as we both stared into our laptops.

"Shit. It's nothing to tell. She called me and was all apologetic about not telling me the truth. I wasn't even listening to her like that. Her reaction was way too light for somebody that almost had me killed. I'm cool on her."

"Good for you," she said. I didn't say anything back.

"You deserve somebody better." This time she looked up over her laptop at me. She was sitting on the loveseat opposite of the larger couch. I was sitting at the desk, laid back in the plush desk chair.

Usually, I would take her words at face value but this time her body language was saying more than her words.

"Somebody like who?" I probed still looking into my laptop. Keeping the conversation going but light.

"I don't know…" she started, then paused. "Somebody better is all I'm saying." She tucked her straightened hair behind her ear, a nervous habit she would do because she didn't know what to do with her hands.

"Define better." I felt like I was picking up what she was throwing out but she wasn't exactly saying anything. So, I continued to probe.

"Better as in… somebody that gets you. That understands what kind of person you are and what motivates you and what you need every day in order to be your best self."

She was sitting on the loveseat Indian-style with her laptop placed on top of her folded legs. She was wearing some slick purple pajama shorts and a white tank top. I never really paid that much attention to Taylor's vibe. I did know what she looked like and had checked her out when I first hired her. I remembered the day she came into my old studio back in Miami, I wasn't immediately turned on, mostly because she was just slim and modest. I thought, "Yea that's a face I don't mind looking at every day. She's what I would call undeniably pretty. Nobody with two working eyes would ever say otherwise. Over the years, she started to grow into that slim body and after many years of my swag rubbing off on her, she found her own drip. She had really fully pink lips, her bottom lip lighter than her top; her eyes were wide but they were overshadowed by her long ass eyelashes, her nose sat perfectly in the center of her face, teeth straight and white, and she always wore her hair in a straightened bob. I always thought she was pretty.

"Why you staring at me like that?" She broke

my concentration.

I closed my laptop. "Damn I can't look at you," I joked. She laughed.

"I'm just saying I think you pick all the wrong women." She was getting specific now.

"So tell me who is the right one. Cause it sounds like you saying it might be you."

"When did I say that?!" She blushed, smiling.

"Yo body telling on you right now and the fact that you keep doing this nervous thing with your hair. What's up, talk to me?" I got up and walked over to the bar and poured a shot of cognac. Took it to the head.

"Be real. You never thought about me and you?" She was curious.

"Honestly, up until right now, no. I didn't think you fucked with niggas like me. I don't know if I'm your speed." I sat down on the couch directly opposite her.

"Not your speed? Meanwhile, I been keeping up with your whole fucking life for the past five years." That was the first time I ever heard her curse.

She had a point. "Yea you been keeping up with my business. You're good at that."

"Your business and your personal life. Your house is taken care of thanks to me. I shop for you. I give you relationship advice, even after I watch you pick women that are all wrong for you."

She wasn't wrong; she been looking out for me for a minute. I hadn't ever really thought about it until now.

"How you knew they were wrong for me?"

"Danielle was too fucking easy for you, you like a challenge. Dana was too bougie, you like your women a little spicy."

"And what about Taya?" I had to ask.

"She was too well put together for you. Too much alpha personality for one relationship. That was bound to be a mess." She read me.

"So I'ma ask you again. Who is the right one?" I wanted her to say it to me; this back in forth we were having was piquing my interest.

"It might be me. I'm down to earth, got enough business acumen but ain't tryna be the next CEO of anything, and for damn sure never gave you easy access to this pussy."

I was shocked she was even talking to me like this. We've never had a conversation like this. I shifted my meat in my pants to just to make sure I wasn't too forward but I was most definitely turned on. Then, I thought about it, if I fucked my assistant, there was no way to come back from that. I don't know if I could find anybody else like her.

"Anyway, we have a long day ahead of us tomorrow. I'm going to bed." She closed her laptop and went into her separate bedroom. I watched her walk away.

It took me two minutes and an extra shot before I decided I knew what I wanted to do.

I went into Taylor's room, pulled back the cover, and slid my body right up against the front of her. I wrapped her top leg around my body and she shifted comfortably into my embrace. Without any hesitation, I pressed my lips against hers softly and gently, pulling her bottom lip between mine then repeating. She was soft as fuck. Her whole body felt like body butter and she smelled like cocoa. Both our eyes closed as I explored all of her body with my hands. Her soft ass was small put plush, I gripped at her tiny waist and ran my thumbs over her nipples that sat erect on top of her large breasts.

I can't believe I hadn't already tried her. But, then, I remembered how much respect I had for her and how I didn't immediately see her as some pussy.

I pulled my lips from hers. "I don't know if we should do this." *Did I just say that?* Cause my dick was in full disagreement.

She sat up on her elbow. She looked at me deep into my eyes, the moonlight lighting up her face. "Why not? I'm not your type?"

She was skeptical but the truth was she wasn't. Not even close but that made me want her even more.

"Nah. It's not that. You sure this is what you wanna do?" I touched her chin.

She looked off, thinking about it.

"There's nobody on this planet I love more than you." She said it with so much confidence that I didn't even know how to react.

I took her words for face value and got lost inside our embrace. Gliding my lips all over her body as she completely submitted to me. She was so small I could easily move her around, putting her into any position I wanted. I used that to my advantage, finding every position I like and, then, deep stroking her insides. No condom, it was just me and her until I was forced to pull out.

35

SHOWTIME
Taya

I flew right into Atlanta on the day of the event. By the time my plane landed, it was T-minus three hours before the show started. Which meant I had one hundred and eighty minutes of nonstop movement ahead of me. This was the type of moment I lived for.

Asya arrived at the same time as me. We were planning to fly back to Austin after the show so we arrived already fitted, suited, and booted. We both rocked custom-tailored fitted suits from our favorite retailers. I had on YSL booties that were stylish and comfortable and Asya wore red bottom flats. Both

245

equally professional and fine. I carried a large designer handbag with my phone, laptop, and change of outfit for the plane back; Asya did the same.

Once we arrived at the venue we had a little less than two hours to make sure everything was where it needed to be. I sent Shelly down days in advance as the person to make everything happen. I knew her forward personality wouldn't let me down; when I entered backstage I heard her barking orders from down the corridor, *that's my girl.*

"Oh, Miss Taya. You've arrived. Good. Let me check that off my list." She looked down at her iPad.

"On time, per usual." I was short. "What's left to do?"

"We're putting the last few touches on the stage now. There's not really anything else to do. But you do have a meeting in five with the PR team. They have a camera crew with them as well. I sent over your speaker notes last night. They will likely interview you."

"Yep, I'm ready. Where's Michael?" I looked up from my phone.

"Oh, perfect, there, Mr. Smell Good goes." She pointed to Mike and Taylor who were both just arriving at the venue.

I greeted Taylor properly. "Is he ready?" I spoke to her directly.

"Yep. Just like you asked, all prepped," she confirmed.

"Good. Then, it's showtime." I handed Shelly my bag. "Take care of this for me. I'll see you when the show starts. Asya you're with us."

We headed to the media room.

There were two things that I wanted to accomplish with this media coverage: first, I wanted the press to run the re-edited footage of Mike's boy's trip to Cabo. The goal here is to actually paint Mike as a relatable owner. I'm sure they would have questions about the content, that's why I had Taylor prep Mike. Second, we needed to not only make Mike look good but our business as well, and that's why I brought Asya.

"Hello everyone," I shouted upon entering the room. Everyone turned to face me. The cameras started rolling. "Glad you all could make it. This is, without a doubt, the biggest show you will cover this year. Michael Keith, CEO of Shut It Down Records is hosting the biggest Hip-Hop, R & B mashup concert the A has ever seen. Before you start your questions allow us to appropriately kick it off." I invited everyone to take their seats.

The room was set up press conference style, just as I requested. There was a green screen in the back for intimate one on one interviews which would follow our opener.

Asya and I took the podium. Mike stood off to the side, just as I laid out in the plans to Taylor.

"Asya Young, MBA Engineering and Dev Ops, representing Vuu: Software and Media Firm. I'd like to welcome you all to the first digital media project since our inception, showcasing the talents of those that represent our esteemed business. We set out to…" Asya

delivered that speech that I wrote for her introducing
our business and principles of operating. She nailed that
shit with poised perfection. After she finished, we
switched spots.

"As you all are already familiar, I am Taya
Roberts. With pleasure, I want to introduce you all to
the face of Shut It Down Records, a business that is
known for top-notch AR services and providing some
of the hottest talent in the country. But, before I give
the stage to Michael Keith, CEO, let's run his
campaign."

The lights in the room dimmed and the screen
behind me ascended. I stepped to the side, grabbing
Mike's arm, guiding him along. He looked nervous but I
wasn't.

The video played, starting exactly how it
originally began. Mike shot me a sharp look. I smiled. I
could tell he was losing trust in me with every second
the video played.

Halfway through the Cabo footage, the video
cut to an interview with Vance. "Mike is a real one. He
party like us, keep it real with us, make plays with us…
he makes sure the whole squad eats." Vance's audio
continued to play as the video shifted to a B-roll of
Mike in the Vuu office. "But at the end of the day, Mike
is all about his business. We don't call him Money Mike
because he makes money, we call him that because he
makes sure we all get it. A little bit of business with a
little bit of pleasure."

The video fades to black and then Mike took
the podium. He delivered the media speech just as I

wrote it.

And, just like that, we solved our media problem and I crystallized my informal brand: The Marketing Tycoon.

The show started right on time after thousands and thousands of hip-hop heads piled into the venue looking to see their favorite southern artists. Some of the biggest names in the city showed up. All the artists that I personally invited came to greet me backstage with warm hugs and gifts and showered me with compliments. They made me miss the Nightlife.

All of Mike's guests were your typical trap, gangsta rappers. The few that I didn't know flirted with me after a quick intro. Mike watched in the background but he didn't really care. I think he was mostly happy that his show was blowing up and that his new studio was already being booked.

After Mike introduced Shut It Down Atlanta to the whole city, the production team turned the speakers up and we had all of Georgia rocking.

"You pulled this off better than anybody could expect." Mike and I finally had a moment to talk backstage.

"You should know by now not to ever doubt me."

"Taya." He grabbed my hand. "I don't know what the fuck I was ever thinking not holding you to the standard that you deserved. I was blessed to have the opportunity to get close to you. I fucked that up and still, you helped me pull off something so important to me." He was the most sincere I had ever seen him. "I mean this with all my soul, if and when you ever need me I got you. I don't care what it is. Money Mike got you. You ain't never gotta ask." He hugged me tightly.

I was warm inside. I was on the fence about telling him about the stunt that Winsdale tried to pull on him and making him feel bad about ever forsaking me. But his sincere words touch the core of my heart and I melted. I hugged him back and nodded with a smile because if I responded I might have shed a tear.

Asya and I cut out early to make our flight back to Austin and sleep quietly in our lakeside home.

36

BLACK TIE AFFAIR
Taya

Our country club hosted their annual Black Tie Affair. This year's theme: *Centennial Lifestyle*. I wore what was probably the sexiest garment I've ever draped over my body. A bold, matte black, form-fitting spandex dress with soft sheer underlining and a sheer tutu puff as wide as my shoulders accompanied by six-inch red bottom stiletto pumps. My face looked like it was beat by the Goddess Apollonia herself. Smoky eyelid, thick lashes, red matte lipstick, and the slickest bun with a fluffy top that the country club had ever seen.

On my arm, I wore Callum. He was also styled by me. Men's GQ only, fresh fade, clean face, and he smelled good. He escorted me out of our Bentley courier. Asya and her date pulled up right behind us. We glided up the stairs to the front door, accepting the attention of the invited media platforms and camera crews.

The Black Tie Affair was a charity fundraiser and while we all knew the purpose was to raise money everyone in attendance used it as an excuse to get dressed up. The best of the best were out showing off and flaunting their cash. Wearing every name brand under the sun, diamonds galore, and stepping out of the most luxurious cars one after the other. We fit right in.

"You are wearing this dress." Callum leaned closely to my face, whispering in my ear as we posed for our last photo before entering the venue. I smiled and posed. He wasn't wrong.

Truth was he was wearing the fuck out of his tux and I couldn't wait to get his ass back to his house and wear him out in his king-sized bed.

"Miss Roberts, a delight to see you, my dear." Just my luck the first white woman I ran into was Catherine Winsdale.

"Why I knew I would see such a prestigious woman at a high-class event." I was just as flattering. I absolutely knew I would run into her. "Have you met my partner? Callum, meet thee Catherine Winsdale."

I could tell he was recalling all the stories I told about her. She extended her hand and Callum, being the gentleman that he is, greeted the back of her hand with a gentle kiss. She accepted his gesture with a smile.

"Can I talk to you privately? In the back? In my office?"

I had no idea she had an office at the country club but I wasn't surprised. "Callum, I'll be right back. The bar is there." I pointed to give him a starting place.

252

He nodded as I walked away following Winsdale.

"What the fuck do you think you're doing?" It was the first thing she said after closing the door to her office. Lucky for her I wasn't surprised.

Her small but cute office was in the back of the club with a view of the golf course. I folded my arms and leaned against her desk for support. I smiled. "Wow. Why the discourse?" I remained composed.

"You filed a lawsuit against me?" She was furious. I see my paperwork from Brandon got around to her, finally.

"No. I did not. However, I did go on record to request the percentage of Vuu I gave you at the beginning of our partnership. If you don't want to comply with my request a lawsuit might possibly be filled," I explained.

"That was a deal between the two of us."

"True. A deal you forced me into because I had no choice. But now that I have new information I think we can renegotiate."

"New information? About what? Where?"

"Malpractice mostly. I don't know if you forget but you advised me to throw Michael Keith under the bus. You broke the protection of client confidentiality the moment you did that."

"I told you nothing!"

I smiled. "Except you told me everything about his business model. You even told me exactly how I could undercut him for my own financial gain. Pretty sure that classifies as a client confidentiality breach. We could see about it in court. It's up to you. Or you could give me back my shares and we can call it even. Either way."

"Taya, I underestimated you." She was honest.

"More than you know." She had no idea I already negotiated purchasing shares of his company with Mike and that I was coming full force for her powerhouse. But she didn't need to know any of that just yet.

"Nice doing business with you, Catherine," I spoke on my way out of her office. I could tell she was done with the conversation and I was ready to get back to the party.

By the time I came back into the picture, the party was in full swing. A live violinist played some of the smoothest jazz music until Callum had a few drinks and took over the piano. He changed the vibe from slow elevator music to smooth rhythm and blues and the violinist followed suit. He was so talented, playing some of our favorites. I stared at him from across the room, watching him get into his groove. He was so effortless with the moods he could create. I was forever learning something new about him; I knew he was a musician but did not know he played the piano. *I bet he can sing too.*

Callum gave up the piano after coaching the actual pianist on the right vibes to set then he joined me in the corner. He reached for my hand and pulled me close, wrapping his left arm around my body while continuing to hold my free hand with his right.

"I needed to make sure I got a dance with the only woman I can see in this room." He stared deeply into my eyes, looking down on me as I willingly allowed him to own the direction of my movements.

"I was wondering when you would remember I was alive." I played.

"That's something I could never forget." He was smooth and, by now, so comfortable around me that things he said just rolled off his tongue.

He pulled me onto the dance floor, keeping me close to him. We glided across the dance floor as if no one was around; engulfed in each other's presence. There was literally no place I would have rather been than right where I was.

About the Author

A passionate writer. Avid Blogger. Former Radio Host. Entrepreneur. HBCU graduate.

An overindulgent personality, a passion for others stories and an incredibly carefree attitude are the writer components that make up Shawn Flossy. As she delivers her latest piece, *Taya's Plight*, Shawn reminds us why we love reading stories about people who don't always have it one hundred percent together. She's known for her straightforward blunt style that is not only relatable but fun to read.

Shawn is a self-published author who founded PURP Publications. Before venturing into her first novel, *The Nightlife Chronicles*, Shawn was known for her viral erotic late night blog that spiraled into her authorship. As a former internet radio host, she learned to lean into the part of her personality that she always believed to be "too outspoken." With more ventures on the horizon, Shawn releases the follow up to *The Nightlife Chronicles*. A story about growth, evolution, and grace.

A PURP Publications Original